# He Was Just A Man...

In a Pierce Brosnan/Antonio Banderas kind of way. His flashing black eyes matched the color of his hair, which he wore rakishly long and combed back from a stunning, masculine face. Sun-tanned cheeks dimpled with saint or sinner charm. His wide brow and strong jaw were classically and unapologetically male.

A crescent-shaped scar cut into his left eyebrow— his one concession to imperfection. It lent a vulnerability that was completely at odds with his overall air of confidence that practically purred:

*I like my women hot.*

*Lady, if I make up my mind to have you, you don't stand a chance on God's green earth of resisting....*

Dear Reader,

Thanks for choosing Silhouette Desire, *the* place to find passionate, powerful and provocative love stories. We're starting off the month in style with Diana Palmer's *Man in Control,* a LONG, TALL TEXANS story and the author's 100th book! Congratulations, Diana, and thank you so much for each and every one of your wonderful stories.

Our continuing series DYNASTIES: THE BARONES is back this month with Anne Marie Winston's thrilling tale *Born To Be Wild.* And Cindy Gerard gives us a fabulous story about a woman who finds romance at her best friend's wedding, in *Tempting the Tycoon.* Weddings seem to be the place to meet a romantic partner (note to self: get invited to more weddings), as we find in Shawna Delacorte's *Having the Best Man's Baby.*

Also this month, Kathie DeNosky is back with another title in her ongoing ranching series—don't miss *Lonetree Ranchers: Morgan* and watch for the final story in this trilogy coming in December. Finally, welcome back the wonderful Emilie Rose with *Cowboy's Million-Dollar Secret,* a fantastic story about a man who inherits much more than he ever expected.

More passion to you!

*Melissa Jeglinski*

Melissa Jeglinski
Senior Editor
Silhouette Desire

Please address questions and book requests to:
Silhouette Reader Service
U.S.: 3010 Walden Ave., P.O. Box 1325, Buffalo, NY 14269
Canadian: P.O. Box 609, Fort Erie, Ont. L2A 5X3

# Tempting the Tycoon

## CINDY GERARD

Silhouette® Desire®

Published by Silhouette Books

America's Publisher of Contemporary Romance

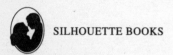

**SILHOUETTE BOOKS**

ISBN 0-373-76539-8

TEMPTING THE TYCOON

Visit Silhouette at www.eHarlequin.com

**Printed in U.S.A.**

## CINDY GERARD

Two RITA® Award nominations and a National Reader's Choice Award are among the many highlights of this #1 bestselling writer's career. As one reviewer put it, "Cindy Gerard provides everything romance readers want in a love story—passion, gut-wrenching emotion, intriguing characters and a captivating plot. This storyteller extraordinaire delivers all of this and more!"

Cindy and her husband, Tom, live in the Midwest on a minifarm with quarter horses, cats and two very spoiled dogs. When she's not writing, she enjoys reading, traveling and spending time at their cabin in northern Minnesota unwinding with family and friends. Cindy loves to hear from her readers and invites you to visit her Web site at www.cindygerard.com.

This book is dedicated to my
intrepid Florida connections, Susan and Jim Connell.
I love you guys!

And to Glenna—
What can I say? You're always there for me.

# One

---

**W**ell, *this* wasn't supposed to happen. She was *not* supposed to be affected. Not like this anyway. Not by a man like him.

Brows pinched in concern, Rachael Matthews fought to ignore the arc of pure and instant attraction that zipped through her blood like a bullet the moment she looked into Nate McGrory's eyes. Wielding her maid-of-honor bouquet like a makeshift shield, she clung to cool reserve and forced herself to hold the best man's gaze as he met her at the center aisle of the church wearing a crooked and way too confident grin.

He was, after all, just a man. Just a man in a Pierce Brosnan/Antonio Bandares sort of way.

All right. She'd give herself a little latitude. What woman wouldn't have a strong reaction? Just look at him.

His flashing brown eyes matched the color of the perfectly styled hair he wore rakishly long and combed straight back from a stunning, masculine face. Contoured, suntanned cheeks dimpled with saint or sinner charm. His straight blade of a nose, wide brow and strong jaw were classically and unapologetically male. A crescent-shaped scar cut into his left eyebrow, just beyond the arc toward his temple—his one concession to imperfection. It should have messed up his incredible face. Instead, it lent a suggestion of vulnerability that was completely at odds with an overall air of confidence that practically purred, *Since you asked, yeah, I am master of my domain—but not to worry—I rule with a kind and gentle hand. And oh, by the way—I like my women hot.*

Okay. That snapped things back into perspective. Arrogance. The man oozed it, a fact that finally nudged Rachael back to her senses with a barely suppressed snort. Oh, yeah. She knew his type. Too well. High-gloss, high-maintenance and way more trouble than they were worth.

When she offered little more than a clipped nod, he widened his killer smile with a look relaying increased interest, along with a clear message. *We meet at last. Let's get these two married and then we definitely need to get to know each other.*

For Karen's sake and for the sake of the two-hundred-odd guests filling the pews and waiting with anticipatory smiles for the main feature—the bride and groom—Rachael made sure her return smile was polite, but about 98.6 degrees cooler than his. A careful lift of her brow did a little speaking, too, though, spelling it out for him, she hoped, *Yeah, sure, whatever.*

He laughed at her.

Oh, not out loud, but with those speaking eyes again—the ones that leveled an unmistakable challenge. *Lady, if I make my mind up to have you, you don't stand a chance on God's green earth of resisting.*

To arrogance, she added egomania.

Well, he might be arrogant, but she, evidently, was an airhead to let herself be affected by him this way. Forget it. This—whatever *this* was, flashing between her and this man she had never officially met—was *not* going to happen. Not only didn't she have the time, she didn't have the patience. Or really, let's face it, she didn't have the inclination. Life was good just the way it was.

Maybe the pressure of planning her best friend's wedding had finally gotten to her. She'd mapped out this day step by meticulous step for Karen. It's what she did. Planning weddings was her career—and for the past several years it had also been her life. But this was Karen—her best friend—so Rachael was that much more invested in the outcome. She wanted everything to be perfect, had done everything in her power to make sure it was. The flowers, the music, the reception later at the Royal Palms Hotel where she operated Brides Unlimited—she'd personally seen to every last detail.

So far, it *was* perfect. And Karen looked beautiful. Thoughts about the glow on her face broke through Rachael's tension and tapped hard on what was left of her romantic streak. The one that, despite several attempts to drown it in a sea of turbulent, shipwrecked relationships, had decided to bob stubbornly to the surface for one final gasp before sinking to be lost forever to the deep just because she'd finally met Nate McGrory.

She started a little when he offered his arm, but recovered and, squaring her shoulders, took it. She could do this. No big deal. It was just the shock of finally seeing him in the flesh after all of Karen's hype that had gotten her going.

"Rachael, I'm telling you," Karen had insisted on one of the rare days, given their busy schedules, when they'd had a chance to get together for a little shopping and catching up last month, "just wait until you meet him."

They'd been lunching at a table on the brick sidewalk at Pescatore, a little pocket of West Palm Beach charm nestled on the corner of Clematis and Narcissus. Fountains flowed in the background, birds sang, exotic Florida flowers bloomed in a riot of intoxicating fragrance and color.

Karen had been blooming, too. They'd just bought her bridal veil—finally—and Karen was extolling the princely virtues of Sam's college fraternity brother, Nate McGrory, a hotshot millionaire lawyer from Miami who would fly in for the wedding at the eleventh hour on his private jet.

"I mean it," Karen had continued emphatically. "If I wasn't so in love with Sam, I'd be boogying on that dance floor myself. Got to be that blend of Irish-Latino blood running through his veins. Rach—I am not exaggerating when I tell you that this guy is not only charming and loaded, he's heart-stopping, to-die-for gorgeous.''

"So are hibiscus blooms and they last for…what? A day?'' Rachael had lifted her glass of merlot, waggling it in warning. "I'm really not interested.''

"But he's so perfect,'' Karen insisted.

"Sweetie, I don't care if he's Ben Affleck, Donald Trump and red-hot Latin lover all rolled into one tidy little testosterone-wrapped package. Karen, please. Get married. Have a great life, but stop trying to couple me up with someone. I've got everything I need to make me happy. Good friends and a great job.''

Why couldn't her friends accept that her life really was fine exactly the way it was? She was productive, successful and self-contained—even if she sometimes fought a niggling notion that there was something more, something out there that eluded her. Something she should be entitled to and didn't have.

Shaking off her thoughts, she tuned back into the minister then cut an uneasy glance toward Nate McGrory.

Grudgingly, Rachael admitted that Karen had delivered on her hype. Mr. Perfect was, indeed, perfect in a black, cutaway tux that made his shoulders look as wide as the intracoastal waterway. Standing at parade rest at Sam's side—very tall, darkly, dangerously handsome—he listened intently as the minister went about his business of joining Karen and Sam as man and wife.

And, she realized with a muffled groan, she'd just spent the bulk of the wedding ceremony ogling him.

Let's blame it on the shoes, shall we? Since she

hadn't wanted to look like a munchkin—she was five-three stacked against Karen and Kim's willowy five-eight and five-nine respectively—she'd opted for four-inch heels. Couple the altitude issue with the pointed-toe factor and the darn shoes must have cut off the blood flow to her brain—pooled it somewhere in the vicinity of her libido, which she'd put in mothballs a couple of years ago and which did not do her thinking for her.

"…I now pronounce you man and wife."

The minister's words brought Rachael back to the reason they were all here.

"Ladies and gentlemen…it is with great pleasure that I present to you Mr. and Mrs. Samuel Lathrop."

Appreciative applause echoed through the church, bounced softly off the stained-glass windows, caromed up then down from the vaulted ceiling and cavernous outer walls as the newlyweds sealed their vows with a kiss that was chaste enough to satisfy the clergy but enthusiastic enough to win a chuckle or two from the congregation. And a knowing wink from the best man, aimed directly at her.

Throwing all of her enthusiasm into Karen and Sam's happiness, she pretended not to notice. And then she pretended she had this puzzling reaction to Nate McGrory under control. A tough trick considering her knees had just turned to mush.

She forced a bright smile that she hoped expressed how truly thrilled she was for Karen and Sam. Then she gritted her teeth as Mr. Wonderful laughed again, sort of a *Fight it if you can, babe, laugh, but I'm gonna getcha.*

She met his eyes as she took his arm and, following the bride and groom down the aisle, delivered her own message. *In your dreams, billionaire boy.*

# Two

"**I** want to be loved like that," Kim Clancy murmured with a wistful sigh as she sat back in her chair at a table flanking the Isle of Paradise Ballroom on the Royal Palms' sixth floor.

Sitting beside Kim, Rachael toyed with the trailing pewter and burgundy ribbons of her bridesmaid's bouquet. All around them, couples danced and laughed—most notably, the starry-eyed bride and groom.

While the pink of the crepe bridesmaids' dresses was a soft complement to Kim's rosy complexion and jet-black hair, Rachael was afraid she hadn't fared as well. In her opinion, green-eyed redheads and hollyhock pink were about as compatible as snowboarding and Jamaica—no matter that the hot glances she'd been dodging all night from Nate McGrory said he more than liked the way she was packaged.

Setting aside her bouquet to systematically shred a paper cocktail napkin with Karen's and Sam's names and wedding date embossed in elaborate gold script, Rachael dragged her thoughts away from the unsettling attention she'd been getting from the best man for the bulk of the evening. She angled Kim a bland look. "I don't want to burst your bubble, Kimmie, but love like that only happens in movies, songs and romance novels."

Okay—and maybe sometimes in real life, she admitted to herself. It just didn't happen in *her* life. Cupping her chin in her palm, she sighed deeply as Karen and Sam waltzed by, eyes only for each other, Karen's antique satin and lace wedding dress swirling around them like a misty cloud.

"I can't believe you aren't happy for Karen."

"Oh, honey, you know I'm happy for her," Rachael assured Kim, who was obviously a little perturbed by Rachael's jaundiced perspective. "Sam's a great guy, but so help me, if he ever hurts her—"

"For heaven's sake. He's not gonna hurt her."

"We'll see."

Kim shook her head. Delicate pink baby roses and wispy sprigs of baby's breath surrounding Kim's upswept black curls fluttered with the motion, reminding Rachael that her hair, too, was wreathed in flowers. On Kimmie they looked elegant. Rachael was pretty sure, however, that despite all attempts to gather her own straight shoulder-length bob up onto her head and encircle it with blossoms, she looked more as if she'd fallen into a patch of wilted weeds than like a wood nymph adorned with wildflowers—which was how the proudly beaming hairdresser had described the result of his labors.

"Don't your shoulders get tired," Kim asked, "what with the weight of that cynicism bearing down on you all the time?"

Rachael lifted a flute of flat, lukewarm champagne. "I don't make the rules. I just observe them."

"You're gonna fall in love for real some day. I, for one, can't wait to watch it happen."

Rachael sipped, swallowed, then shook her head. The motion sent a tendril of red hair in a downward slide. She felt it on her bare nape and attempted to tuck it back up into her circlet of flowers. "Read the book. Saw the movie. No need to play the part, so don't hold your breath on my account because it's never gonna happen."

"Never's a long time, Rach," Kim said softly.

Rachael knew about long times. It had been a long time, for instance, since she'd felt she could count on anyone but herself. She was fine with that. She was independent and proud of it—plus the mere thought of committing to one person, depending on one person—well, it just wasn't something she felt comfortable with.

Kimmie and Karen both accused her of having "issues" with trust. This was not news. She admitted it. They were right. But she didn't necessarily see anything wrong with being careful. Or with being single and content with it.

She forced a smile for Kim, who was always and forever an optimist. Rachael forgave her for it because she loved her like a sister. And because she understood that Kim had no reason not to believe in love and romance and family-ever-after. Rachael, on the other hand, knew a little too much about that great American fallacy. She thought fleetingly about her mother and wondered how she'd had the strength to carry on given all she'd been through.

"Just give me good old-fashioned lust," she said, breaking away from her thoughts. "At least it's honest."

"Yeah, right." Kim snorted. "Like you'd ever go for that kind of arrangement."

Okay. So Kim knew her well. Rachael didn't do casual sex. Every once in a while, though, she wished she could be one of those women who could take the sex without the commitment she needed to make it worth the effort. It seemed to work just fine for the guys.

"You never know," Rachael said with false bravado, "maybe I'll turn over a new leaf. Go for the gusto without the grief."

"A new leaf, huh? Better make it a fig leaf, 'cause it looks like you just might get a chance to put the new you front and center."

When Rachael shot her a curious look, Kim nodded in the direction of the man dodging couples on the dance floor and heading toward them. "Hunk alert at six o'clock. Hubba-hubba-holy-cow-what-a-man. If you don't want him, put in a word for me, would you?"

Rachael felt her shoulders stiffen. She'd felt Nate McGrory's hot gaze on her all night—in the reception line after the ceremony, in the limo on the way here and at the bride's table during dinner. He hadn't slacked off since the band had played their first chords three hours ago. Except for the traditional dance when the best man and maid of honor were expected to dance together, she'd managed to keep herself occupied with details surrounding the reception and him at a distance.

"Ladies," he said, by way of greeting, his killer smile locked and loaded.

Rachael tried to look bored, all the while thinking of how he'd smelled—like musk and spice and something exotically sexy—when they'd danced that one, seemingly endless dance. She tried not to remember the heat of his broad hand spread wide across her back, or how protected and small she'd felt when his chin had brushed the top of her head and his warm breath had stirred the flowers in her hair and made her flush warm all over. She tried—really, she tried—not to remember the feel of his thighs brushing hers, her breasts pressed against the broad chest beneath his tuxedo jacket.

"You're both looking very…pink tonight," he observed dryly as he sat down in the empty chair beside Rachael.

Rachael toyed with the mints on the plate beside her untouched wedding cake and hoped the little bump, bump, bump of her heart against the left cup of her merry widow didn't bump her right out of her dress.

"Why yes, we are," she said with false brightness, "and it's only because Karen would walk over hot coals for us that we agreed to wearing these—"

"Very pink dresses?" he supplied with a cheeky grin she chose not to return.

"Close enough."

His smile mellowed into something intimate and way too friendly as he propped an elbow lazily on the table and leaned directly into her field of vision. Rachael stubbornly held his gaze in a game attempt to let him know he didn't affect her. She thought she'd managed a pretty good job of it, too—until he poked an index finger into the frosting on her untouched cake, studied it idly, then brought it to his mouth.

She swallowed, her mouth dust-dry, as he sucked it slowly off his finger.

"Good."

The single word, uttered in his deep voice, rubbed along her senses like lush velvet. Heat flooded every freckle from her breast to her hairline. She jerked her gaze away.

Good God.

"So, how's it going, Nate?" This from Kim, who was kicking Rachael under the table in a bid, no doubt, for her to lose the frown and a show a little interest.

"Not so good," he said, and Rachael was peripherally aware of his gaze drifting along her flushed face to the curve of her jaw, slowly working its way lower, to her bare shoulder and along the low-cut line of her dress. "This is one of my favorite songs," he said with just enough pout in his voice to make it sound even sexier, "and here I am—no one to dance with."

Hyperaware of the direction his gaze had taken, Rachael toyed with the stem of her champagne flute and paid undue attention to the small stack of shredded napkin piled in front of her.

"Give a guy a break?" he asked with the sultry charm of a prince—or a sultan. "Dance with me?"

She was about to utter a polite but firm no thank-you, when she looked up and realized he'd extended his invitation to Kim.

She snapped her mouth shut, carefully bit back her surprise and gave an uncertain and confused Kim a nod of encouragement. "Go ahead. Dance your socks off."

With a puzzled look, Kim followed the best man's lead onto the dance floor then floated into his open arms.

Well, Rachael thought as she watched them meld into the crowd. That was a relief. A huge relief that he'd finally gotten the hint and backed off. And she didn't feel confused, or rejected, or let down that it was Kim he'd come for, not her. She didn't feel any of those things.

Not even when they danced the next three dances, their dark heads together, laughing, talking, absorbed with each other and oblivious to anyone else in the room. Totally oblivious to her when she rose and left the ballroom unobserved to double-check on the hundreds of white balloons and baskets of heart-shaped confetti that were to be released at midnight, just before the happy couple left for their honeymoon.

It didn't bother her—not even a little bit.

From the dance floor, Nate watched over Kim's shoulder as Rachael Matthews sneaked out of the ballroom like a thief taking a hike with the family jewels. He wasn't sure why he was so intrigued by the little green-eyed redhead. Hell. For the better part of the day she'd regarded him the way she would a piece of meat that had been left out in the sun too long.

He grinned and shook his head. He was used to excessive reactions from women. Avoidance wasn't one of them. He wasn't conceited but he wasn't blind, either. He wasn't oblivious to his looks—not his fault or his doing that he came from a great gene pool. Also not his doing that the lure of his family fortune and his unsolicited reputation as one of Florida's most eligible bachelors netted him his fair share of female attention. And yeah, to a degree, he liked that attention—would even admit he'd used his looks and his financial and social position to his advantage from time to time.

Not that any of it would get him anywhere with Rachael. Her reaction continued to both amuse and stymie him. Since he hadn't known her long enough to offend her, he had to figure it was the lady herself who had the problem—and he'd decided he'd like nothing better than playing the role of problem solver.

"Okay, you can cut the pretense now."

Nate swung his gaze down to the pretty woman in his arms. "Excuse me?"

Kim Clancy smiled sweetly. "She's gone. Rachael," she said, nodding to the double doors where Nate had last seen her. "She's gone, so you can get down to the nitty-gritty. What do you want to know about her?"

One corner of his mouth tipped up. Busted. "Am I that transparent?"

"Clear as plastic wrap," she said with that same cheerful smile.

"I'm sorry. Do you mind?"

Kim met his eyes with frank candor. "What I would mind is for Rachael to get hurt. She's not a player, Nate. Beneath the brass and barbwire, she's fragile.

"So," she continued, her gaze assessing as the slow dance came to an end, "if all you have in mind is a hit-and-run, as her friend, I'd appreciate it if you find another moving target."

He wasn't sure what he had in mind, but target practice wasn't among the options concerning this woman who inspired such loyalty from another woman.

"How about we go somewhere and talk," he said, his hand at the small of her back as he guided Kim off the dance floor.

"About Rachael?"

"What can I say? I think I've got it bad." He grinned at her less-than-sympathetic look. "Be a pal. Tell me something about her that will make it all go away."

# Three

The Monday after Karen's wedding was one of those Mondays Rachael both relished and dreaded. She'd hit the ground running when she'd walked through the ornate revolving doors of the Royal Palms Hotel at seven-fifteen. Now it was close to lunchtime and she hadn't had time to draw a deep breath yet.

She'd barely walked up the stairs—she much preferred them to the elevator—and entered her third-floor office with the breathtaking view of the beach and the Atlantic when Sylvie Baxter started firing questions at her like bullets. Did she remember she had a meeting with the head of a new printing company who wants to pitch his work at 8:30? Was the tasting for the Jenner wedding reception still on for this afternoon or had she dreamed it had been rescheduled? Did Rachael know that Alejandro, the sous chef for the fourth-floor restaurant, had run off with the manager's wife? Don't forget to call the Sanbourns, oh, and Mrs. Buckley is on line one.

Rachael had talked the hotel management into expanding Brides Unlimited—Royal Palms' upscale bridal service—to a full-service wedding operation three years ago. After business had increased by a full twenty percent the first year under her management, she'd asked for and been granted permission to hire an assistant. Sylvie, a sixty-something widow, was Rachael's best ''perk'' yet.

Sylvie'd been on the job for eighteen months now; Rachael couldn't imagine running things without her. And she couldn't imagine herself doing anything else. This job was the single most important thing in her life. It was what she banked on. It was what she believed in.

And her hard work was really paying off. Business just kept getting better. Projections forecasted an additional fifteen-percent rise in clientele for the quarter—possibly thirty-five percent for the year—and it was only March. The year was young.

This day, however, was getting old fast—mostly due to her current phone conversation.

Rachael sat at her desk, her hands steepled in front of her as Mrs. Haden Buckley the third's nasal voice grated through her headset. Gweneth Buckley was a royal pain in the hiney. She also represented her biggest account to date and possibly Brides Unlimited's ticket into the crème de la crème of Palm Beach high society. If Mrs. Buckley liked what Rachael did with her daughter's wedding, word would spread not only among Palm Beach old guard, but among the nouveau riche. Business would grow. And for that reason, Rachael tried to ignore the fact that it was almost eleven-thirty and this was Gweneth's fourth contact of the day requesting changes in the wedding plans.

Rachael adjusted her headset, checked her watch and wondered if she'd have to break her lunch date with Kim. She hadn't seen or spoken with her since Karen's wedding Saturday and some small part of her wanted to hear how she'd made out with Mr. Wonderful. Not that she had any interest in Nate McGrory, but she *was* interested in Kim. Kimmie was romantic and naive and Rachael wanted to hear if he'd given her the total bum's rush before he returned to Miami and his law practice—and the legion of women who followed in his wake like a jetstream if the article she'd stumbled across in *Florida Today* was to be believed.

"Yes, Mrs. Buckley," she agreed pleasantly, "we'll be happy to substitute the Grand Marnier crème brûulée for the mignardises. A fine choice for dessert." At this point she really didn't care if Mrs. Buckley's guests ate the torched custard or the chocolate-dipped fruits, truffles, European cookies and biscotti. She just wanted a firm decision to send to the pastry chef.

"I'm sorry, what?" she asked when she realized she'd zoned out. "Oh, yes. Yes, I've been able to negotiate a contract with Butterflies, Inc., that will meet your budget." As if the Palm Beach Buckleys needed to work with a budget, she thought silently.

She drew a deep breath, then carefully dived in. "Mrs. Buckley, all of your choices have been brilliant—including these adjustments. I understand how perfect you want everything to be. The wedding will be spectacular. Your daughter will look stunning. The guests will be raving about the food for months. We'll be at a point soon, however, where I'll need to send confirmation notices to all the vendors on any last-minute alterations.''

Ten minutes later, she'd finally managed to get off the phone. She was just lifting her headset from her ears when Sylvie rapped a knuckle on her door then poked her head inside.

''Your lunch date's here,'' Sylvie said with a coy grin.

Puzzled by Sylvie's dancing eyes, Rachael eyed her with suspicion. It wasn't like having lunch with Kim was a special occasion. They had a standing Monday date. ''And?''

''And…I thought the light on line one was never going to go out.''

''Mrs. Buckley,'' Rachael said by way of explanation.

''Say no more. Well…um, I'll just…let you go to lunch then,'' Sylvie said brightly.

Rachael didn't have time to contemplate the waggle of Sylvie's eyebrows as she popped her head back out the door.

''Leave it open,'' Rachael called as she rose and tucked her hair behind her ear. ''I'm right behind you.''

She slipped into her royal-blue blazer with the Royal Palms Hotel crest on the breast pocket and straightened her matching skirt. Her head was down and she was digging around in her purse for her sunglasses when she rushed through the door.

"Hurry," she said without looking up. "Let's make a break for it before she calls with another cha—" she stopped midword and midstride, halfway out the outer office door when she saw who was waiting for her in the reception area.

It was *not* Kimmie.

With one hand on the doorjamb, Rachael turned back to Sylvie who cast a speculative glance between her and the man artlessly arranged in a casual slouch in a raspberry-upholstered and chrome chair. A smile as wide as Palm Beach stretched across the face Rachael was mortified to admit she'd dreamed about the past two nights.

Nate McGrory's pricey taupe silk polo shirt hugged his broad shoulders and tapered to his lean hips and long legs covered in tailored black trousers. Casual chic, very masculine—sexy personified. It was a style he wore even better than he had the cutaway tux. Possibly the softly curling chest hair peeking from the open placket at his throat and the deeply tanned and nicely muscled biceps had something to do with it. Possibly she needed to close her mouth before she started drooling. And absolutely she needed to pull herself together.

She shot Sylvie an accusing glare. "Where's Kimmie?"

Sylvie tucked a pencil into her short, stylishly coiffed salt-and-pepper hair and, with a nod, deferred to Nate.

"Regrettably detained," Nate explained as he unfolded all six-plus totally buff feet from the chair. "I volunteered to fill in. Hope it's okay."

She closed her eyes. Let out a breath.

''You know,'' she said, and forced a brittle smile, ''that's very nice of you—really—but I just remembered. I have another appointment outside the office right about now.''

His grin only widened. ''Then I'll drive you.'' He shrugged, a man on an unmistakable mission. ''We can pick up something to eat on the way. Wouldn't want you to miss your lunch.''

His eyes were very dark. His smile was very warm—so were her cheeks and other places she didn't want to think about. And her adolescent physical reactions to him were really starting to tick her off.

''Sylvie—could you check my calendar, please? I may have misspoken. I think my appointment is here at the hotel, after all. In five minutes, right?'' she added, meaning, *Go with this and lie for me or you will live to regret it.*

Sylvie blinked and affected a smile as innocent as a baby's. ''Nope. All I've got down for you is lunch with Kim.''

*You will die tomorrow,* Rachael assured Sylvie with a look that had no affect on her whatsoever—except to broaden her smug grin.

Behind her, Nate laughed. The sound rumbled through her senses, and to her disgust, jacked up the speed of her heartbeat. ''Come on, Ms. Congeniality. Looks like you're stuck with me. Might just as well give it up and make the best of it. You have no way of knowing this, but it's been rumored that I'm a fun date,'' he added with one of those slashing grins she remembered from the wedding—and from her dreams.

She blinked and clung to her defenses with a slippery grasp. "This is not a date."

"If it makes it easier for you to deal with," he said amiably and touched his hand to the small of her back, "then you just put whatever spin on it you want. Me, I kind of like the idea of it being a—"

"Not a date," she repeated in a clipped tone that she hoped didn't sound as desperate as she suddenly felt.

She shot Sylvie—who was looking far too amused—a dark look. She was enjoying this, damn her. Okay. Enough was enough. This little scenario could play out forever, but she had no intention of being Sylvie's or Nate McGrory's afternoon entertainment as she fumbled around for feeble excuses to get out of going to lunch with him. It was also not a hill, she decided, on which she chose to die. She could do this. She could go to lunch with the man, convince him he was wasting his time and he'd back off. End of story.

"I'll be back by twelve-thirty," she told Sylvie, and, feeling a nearly compulsive need to move away from the warm pressure of his hand at the small of her back, she marched ahead of him out the door.

It wasn't that his touch repulsed her. Just the opposite. That slight but proprietary and wholly male gesture, the barest pressure of his fingertips at the small of her back, had far from repelled her. It had made her shiver—and not because the air conditioning was turned down to iceberg to accommodate Sylvie's hot flashes. No, his touch had nothing to do with making her cold and everything to do with making her feel hot. And edgy. And exposed. And all of that made her feel vulnerable. And that, she decided, was the real kicker and the reason he was throwing her so off guard.

Vulnerable was something she didn't have any inclination to be. Especially not around this man—because this man, she finally admitted, just might have what it took to break down her defenses. This man—with his incredible smile and loyal legion of friends who thought he was the best thing since the microchip—had gotten to her the first time she'd looked into his eyes despite her best attempts to ignore him.

Okay. What, exactly, are you doing here? Nate asked himself as he drove west down Royal Palm Way. Beside him, a very silent Rachael Matthews stared straight ahead, her hands folded primly on her lap.

She sat so stiffly and formally she could have been wearing a police uniform instead of the royal-blue skirt and blazer that were the trademark and standard attire for the Royal Palms Hotel staff. The white blouse and neat red tie knotted securely at her throat were intended to express a chic but professional presence. And, absolutely, they did. Except…the way the short snug skirt and tailored jacket hugged Rachael Matthews's curvy little body undermined the business statement.

She was every inch the luscious little morsel who had looked so pretty in pink at Sam's wedding. In fact, he hadn't been able to get the picture of her wrapped in clingy crepe out of his head. Now he was wondering what kind of underwear the prim and proper Ms. Matthews wore beneath her formfitting uniform. Lace, he was guessing. Something frothy and feminine and sheer and maybe just a little naughty. Something about her shouted sensuality, regardless of how professional she looked.

Lust—a good healthy punch of it—had knocked him for a loop the moment he'd set eyes on her. It still had a hold of him, or he probably wouldn't be here now, beating his head against the brick wall she'd laid with thick mortar and a big trowel, fantasizing about her underwear. The lady had clearly given him the ice-cube shoulder at the wedding Saturday night. She was not interested then—in capital letters. She was not interested now—with exclamation points.

Her reaction didn't negate the fact that he *was* interested—very—not only in the package, but in the person inside it. So what, exactly, did he see in her, since so far she'd snubbed him? Or was that the crux of it? It was embarrassing that most women tripped over themselves getting to him. Not her. To her, he was very resistible. Call him crazy, but he liked that about her.

He tapped a thumb on the steering wheel and braked for a red light. Was that it? Was it the challenge of breaking down her cool reserve? She wasn't reserved with her friends. He'd observed her for the better part of the reception Saturday night. Her touching toast to Karen brought tears to the eyes of most of the women in the room and had a few guys—him among them—clearing the lumps from their throats. How could a woman who obviously had such great capacity to love have sworn off men, as Kim had told him? And how was it that a woman who planned other women's happily-ever-afters didn't see one for herself? There was something sadly ironic in that.

He'd been hoping a heart-to-heart with Kim would cool his jets, but she'd reaffirmed what Sam had already told him. Rachael was a hard-working, make-it-on-her-own kind of girl. Unlucky in love, Kim had said. The look on Rachael's face when she'd accidentally caught Karen's bouquet at the reception had been sheer panic and had spoken volumes. She'd tossed it to Kim like a hot potato.

Had somebody burned her? It would seem that way, but even Kim, who had warmed to the role of matchmaker as the night had worn on, wouldn't give up the details, which only went to show the kind of loyalty Rachael inspired.

He shook his head, knowing he might be fighting a losing battle. Evidently, there was something about Rachael that brought out latent masochistic tendencies, because here he was, strapping on a bull's-eye for a round of target practice and she was just itching to shoot him down. He'd actually hung around in Palm Beach for an extra day for this chance at seeing her again and she'd made it clear—again—that she'd rather spend five minutes in a snake pit than an hour chatting and chewing with him.

He cut her a sideways glance. Grinned in spite of himself. The sun cut across her profile as they breezed down the busy street. She was so pretty.

He checked his rearview mirror and changed lanes. *Pretty* was a simple word for such an intriguing package, but in all honesty, it was the one that fit her best. She wasn't gorgeous, not in the goddess sense, although her huge, wide-set eyes—as green as colored glass and just as bright—sparkled with intelligence and independent pride and were more mesmerizing than any eyes he'd seen gracing a cover of *Vogue.* She wasn't what most people would consider beautiful, although the silky sweep of copper-red hair— that looked so much more natural today falling loose and straight around her shoulders than wrestled into a wreath of flowers—had a stunning effect and made a man itch to feel it sifting through his fingers.

Her mouth was too wide, her lips too full to be considered classically perfect. Her nose was short and sweet and cute. Just like she was. He grinned and figured there'd be death to the man who was stupid enough to call anything about her *cute* to her face. Or *sweet.*

No. Ms. Rachael Matthews did not regard herself as cute. Sophisticated, yes. Professional, absolutely. Dynamic, for a fact. She was all that.

And pretty.

And he was smitten.

Helluva deal.

"I have to be back in forty-five minutes," she informed him stiffly when Royal Palm Way became Okeechobee Boulevard and they continued across the bridge over Lake Worth and into West Palm.

"Slave driver for a boss?" he asked conversationally.

"A very full day."

"Then it's a good thing you're getting out and away from it for a little while. It'll give you an edge for the afternoon."

No response. Not that he'd expected one. He did

get a reaction, however, when he pulled in to a fast-food drive-through line.

She actually smiled, although he could tell she didn't want to.

"So, who have you been talking to?" she asked, her voice just a little less edgy and a little more relaxed.

"Sorry. I never reveal my sources. But I take it they were right? While you look like a caviar-and-truffles kind of girl, deep down you're a closet fast-food junkie."

In answer, she merely tilted her head. "I'll have a number four, please."

He smiled and turned to the squawk box. "Two number fours—and super-size 'em, okay?"

When he turned back to her, she was looking out the passenger window. He didn't have to see her face to know she was still smiling.

Score one for the good guy, he thought smugly and pulled ahead to the pay window.

Things were looking up.


"So, is it just me, or is it lawyers in general you regard as toxic waste?"

He'd driven back across the bridge into Palm Beach and parked at a metered spot along Ocean Boulevard. Rachael had left her jacket in his rented black SUV in deference to the warm March sun. They sat side by side on a bench behind the seawall, facing the ocean, eating a lunch that was sure to send her into a carbo-coma later this afternoon. But not now. Now, all of her senses were revved to warp speed. This man—this man pulled reactions out of her she'd told herself she wasn't going to submit to until she was darn good and ready. Which she wasn't. Not yet. Maybe not ever. She was too busy. Building her career. Proving she didn't need anyone but herself to make her life complete.

She hadn't understood her reaction to him the first time she'd met him. She still didn't understand it. He was too brash, too bold and too confident and way too full of himself. And just like the first moment they'd met, she was far too aware of the unexplained zip of sexual heat arcing between them. And it was just sexual. She didn't know him well enough for there to be anything else. Even this unexplained tug she felt toward him was sexual. Probably.

Damn Karen for making him out to be God's gift and suggesting he might be hers for the taking.

Several yards below them, down the wooden steps and beyond the wrack-strewn sand, a stiff easterly wind had riled the Atlantic into pummeling swells. The lifeguard board posted undertow and man o' war warnings. Oiled bodies lounged or lay here and there on jewel-colored towels, soaking up the Florida sun. Children played in the sand at the base of the rugged rock walls of the jetties while surfers poured into wet suits, straddled their boards and paddled past the lesser waves, waiting for the ultimate ride. Further out, the gleaming white hulls of pricey yachts and the occasional cruise ship dotted the horizon.

Behind them, sidewalk and road traffic buzzed by, adding another level of noise to the surf and the wind and the screech of swooping gulls. And yet, Rachael's world was reduced to the moment and the man who sat beside her, eating his lunch with gusto, apparently oblivious to her discomfort. She didn't want to react to him, but she was filled with that same hyper-awareness she'd experienced at the wedding—aware-ness of his utterly male presence, of his dark eyes dancing over her face, of the way he smelled, like citrus and salt and masculinity.

He'd asked her a question. *Is it just me, or is it lawyers in general you regard as toxic waste?*

Oh, how about—you throw me completely for a loop and I don't know why. Sure. Like she was going to admit that.

Instead of coming clean, she asked a question of her own. "What, exactly, happened to Kim today?"

He popped a French fry into his mouth, chewed, then swallowed as he looked out to sea. She watched, fascinated, in spite of herself, by the way the muscles in his jaw worked, intrigued by the little scar in his brow and the mobile lips that were so quick to smile, so clever and ready to tease.

"Well, I called to ask her if she thought I could talk you into going to lunch with me and she very graciously suggested I substitute for her."

The easy way he said it stirred her anger. "Kim-mie's special," she said, meeting those glittering brown eyes. "She's not someone to play with then throw away."

He looked taken aback, then raised a hand. "Hey— I *like* Kim. She's great."

"Then why did you put the moves on her then turn around and try to make time with me?"

He tilted his head, shook it, then nodded as if un-derstanding had dawned. "You're talking about the reception."

"You looked pretty tight."

"I was pumping her for information about you—which, I might add, she was more than willing to give up."

Oh, she thought. Oh. So *that's* what they'd been about. She didn't want to be pleased by the thought. And she didn't want to be charmed by him. Yet, she was dangerously close to both reactions. "You could have asked me."

"And you would have answered?" He snorted and tossed back another fry. "I don't think so. You ran like a rabbit every time I got within a city block of you."

"I didn't run. I avoided. There's a difference. Most men would take it as a sign I wasn't interested."

He grinned, crooked and disarming, and brushed salt from his fingers. "I'm not most men. And you *are* interested."

No, he wasn't most men, she thought morosely and averted her gaze to the ocean. And she wished he was wrong. She wished she wasn't interested. She didn't have time to be interested. She couldn't afford to be interested.

"I'd like to get to know you, Rachael," he said quietly. "Would that be such a bad thing?"

Like his smile, this sudden sincerity was disarming. She shook her head, determined to stay the course. "Look, Nate—"

He cut her off with the touch of his hand to her cheek. She turned her head slowly and swallowed when he brushed a stray strand of windswept hair away from the corner of her mouth. "What are you afraid of?"

She stood abruptly, balled up the lunch she'd hardly touched, and tossed it in a nearby trash can. She wasn't afraid. Not exactly. She was simply wise. She knew how to protect herself and every instinct she trusted told her she needed to protect herself from him. "Let's just say this isn't a good time for me right now and leave it at that, okay?"

He was quiet for a moment and then she heard him rise. "So when would be a good time?"

When his shadow fell across hers on the sidewalk, she walked the few feet to the seawall and away from him. She stared out at the breakers rolling in, felt the sea salt and wind in her hair. When she sensed him beside her again, she looked up and over her shoulder.

The sun played across the sculpted angles and planes of his strong face as he tugged off his sunglasses then reached down and tugged hers off, too. She quelled the urge to reach up and run her fingers along the scar splitting his eyebrow.

Heartbreak. He was heartbreak waiting to happen and she was too smart to let herself in for the pain he could dole out.

"How long has it been since you were involved with someone?" he asked, settling a hip onto the seawall. With his back to the ocean, he crossed his arms over his chest and watched her face.

"How long?" he persisted softly, his expression so interested and so sincere, she was mortified that she wanted to tell him.

Long enough to know I don't have it in me to open up and give a relationship what it needs. Long enough to know I'm not cut out for couplehood.

She decided the short version was the best. "Long enough."

"Sounds like the perfect time to try again, don't you think?" His voice was very deep, brimming with the suggestion that he thought it was time to explore the possibility with him.

It took everything in her to shake her head. "No. I don't think so."

When his expression pressed for more than that, she relented.

"Look…you're getting way ahead of yourself here, okay?" She felt on the defensive suddenly and, damn him, his earnest look compelled her to say more than she wanted to say. "In the first place, you're moving way too fast. In the second place, I'm not interested. And in case those two didn't do it for you, I don't do well with relationships."

She paused, disturbed to hear the huskiness in her voice, then felt her cheeks flush with embarrassment at her choice of words. *Relationships.* Well, that ought to scare him off. Men like Nate McGrory didn't do relationships. They did flings, affairs, one-night stands. No doubt just breathing the word had him thinking about packing up his toys and, like those who had preceded him, heading for a new playground.

And yet, when she looked up to see if he was searching for the nearest exit, his gaze was intent on her face.

"Why is that?" His voice was so soft she had to strain to hear him above the rush of the wind and the call of the gulls and the traffic breezing by behind them.

"W-why is what?" She'd totally lost the thread of conversation, captivated by the fervency of his gaze.

"Why don't you do well at relationships?"

Nerves had her pushing out a humorless laugh and letting down her guard. Because relationships required something she didn't have in her to give. They required opening up to someone, laying yourself bare. And that just wasn't going to happen. "The usual reasons—too many, too varied and too boring to relate."

"Try me."

She dragged a hand through her hair, drew a bracing breath. "Look, Nate," she said, gathering her composure and turning to fully face him, "this is all very flattering. You're a really gorgeous guy—I'm sure you're very nice, but I'm just not up for any kind of—entanglement," she finally finished, deciding the word covered a plethora of possibilities.

His eyes were very dark as he pushed away from the seawall and cupped her shoulders in his big hands. "All I'm asking is that you think about it. Think about the possibility of an…entanglement," he said with a kind and gently teasing grin.

"And while you're at it," he whispered, watching her face as he lowered his mouth to hers, "think about this."

# Four

Rachael should have seen it coming. She should have sensed, when Nate's strong hands gripped her shoulders and he started pulling her toward him, that he was going to kiss her. And maybe she did. Maybe she did see it coming, and maybe she could have stopped it.

But she didn't. Instead, she stood there, letting the worst possible thing that could happen to her draw her unerringly toward him.

His dark eyes, framed by thick, long lashes, searched her face, offering her the opportunity to pull away as he lowered his head to hers. He would have. He would have backed off if she'd given him the slightest indication. Yet all she could find it in herself to do was stand there and hang on for the ride.

The first touch of his mouth was electric. Softly,

sensuously electric. A mere brush of lips to lips. Not a tentative touch…more of an introduction, a promise, a gentle hello that reawakened the woman's need she'd told herself was not essential in her life. But, oh. She'd been wrong. She'd missed this. She'd missed this illicit little rush of yearning, this sweet quickening of a heartbeat he managed to alter more than any other man had.

His breath fell soft on her cheek as his nose brushed hers in a playful caress, while his mouth continued a tender assault on her defenses.

She heard a sigh, realized it was hers when his lips curved into a smile against her mouth just before he drew her deeply, decisively into his embrace and into a kiss the likes of which she'd never in her life experienced.

Delicious longing, humming passion infused her senses, easing her beyond any protest she might have lodged, spiraling her into an isolated cocoon of sensations too lush to categorize, too consuming to fight.

She wasn't aware of any conscious decision on her part to slip her arms around his waist and lean into him. She was aware only of heat. His. Hers. And of the broad musculature of his chest pressed against her breasts, the lean hardness of his hips meeting hers, the unmistakable and growing ridge of his erection nestled against her tummy.

Before she could react to the shock of it and pull away, he smiled against her mouth again, groaned a husky, "Sorry…that just sort of happens when I'm around you," and eased her into another drugging kiss.

*Intoxicating* was the perfect word for what he was

doing to her. She enjoyed the occasional glass of wine but didn't now and never had indulged in chemical stimulation. Yet drugged was exactly how she felt. Why else would she let down her defenses this way? Why else would she let him play with her mouth…nipping…nudging…testing with the tip of his tongue then shooting sparks through her body in a dizzying rush before he took her mouth again?

Oblivious to her surroundings, she melted into the kiss that was all silky heat and skillful seduction. He opened his mouth wide over hers, coaxed her with gentle but insistent pressure to open up, to let him in, let him taste, let herself feel the wonder of his total possession.

And still, he was never demanding. His tongue played in her mouth, learning her taste, exploring her textures, tempting, teasing, inviting her to do some exploring of her own. She couldn't resist. She followed his tongue as he withdrew, beckoning her to linger along the seam of his lips before delving inside and indulging in the illicit excitement of the experience.

With a deep groan, he changed the angle of his mouth and lifted her, setting her onto the seawall, then made a place for himself between her thighs. Time, place, proximity—they were all lost to her as he made love to her mouth and pressed the now very strong evidence of his physical reaction into the cleft between her legs. His hands spanned her hips, holding the part of her that pulsed with need tight against him.

It was the catcalls that finally penetrated her fog of pleasure. The sound of a skateboard and a trailing, "Hey dude, way to go, man," that finally forced her to open her eyes and snag a tenuous hold on her senses.

She broke the kiss, blinked up into eyes that were slumberous and dark and by all indications, deeply pleased by the turn of events.

He loosened his grip on her hips, slid his hands in a lazy caress to the small of her back and kneaded softly. "Well." He pressed his forehead to hers and smiled into her eyes. "Well, well, well."

She looked like a little bird as she blinked up at him, Nate thought. An adorable, thoroughly kissable, totally rattled little bird. He hadn't meant for it to go this far. He'd only meant to kiss her. Just kiss her. Just initiate a little physical dialogue to open her eyes to possibilities and break the tension that had been building between them.

He hadn't meant to turn it into a marathon session that he'd wanted to go on forever—or until he had her naked somewhere where they could take it to the next level. He hadn't meant to lose himself in her taste or the feel of her breasts pressed against his chest and his erection nestled into the sweet heat between her thighs.

He hadn't meant to do a lot of things. But he hadn't burned this hot this fast since—hell…he didn't know when a woman had flipped his switch this way.

Well, now he knew that one blistering hot kiss from Rachael Matthews—who, he reminded himself smugly, had done a little igniting of her own—was not going to be the sum total of their physical relationship.

Now seemed as good a time as any to make sure she knew it, too. He dove back for another kiss. The quick pressure of her hand on his chest between them stopped him.

"What?" he asked, only a vague interest in what kind of protest she was going to lodge crossing his mind. He didn't really care how much she protested verbally. She'd just shown him how she felt. She wanted this as much as he did. They didn't have to analyze why it was so spontaneous and intense between them. They just had to go with it.

"I don't *do* this," she blurted out, and this time she brought up her other hand to join the one making a half-hearted attempt to push him away. "I don't go around kissing men I hardly know. And I don't make a habit of making a spectacle of myself on a public sidewalk."

He would have felt guilty if he hadn't been so pleased by her rattled admission. And the unflappable Ms. Matthews was definitely rattled. He was doubly pleased that she'd as much as admitted it wasn't just any guy who tripped her trigger. It was him.

"For not *doing* it," he said, feeling another smile slip into place, "you *do* it remarkably well."

"Let me go," she enunciated carefully but without much heat.

In spite of his reluctance, he felt himself smiling again and did as she asked. Besides this fairly constant state of arousal he experienced when he was around her, he found himself doing that a lot. Smiling. Again, he wasn't sure why. Something about her. Something unexpectedly appealing, incredibly sexy and softly vulnerable no matter how businesslike and stern a facade she'd built to hide her true feelings.

It intrigued the hell out of him, this interest he felt

in her. It wasn't just sexual—although, good night, Isadora, the woman messed with his control. It was more. He liked her...hadn't felt this drawn to a woman since Tia.

The thought of Tia gave him pause. He'd been purposefully keeping her out of the equation. Until now. He loved Tia. Always would. The unfortunate fact that he could never have her, kept him from acting on that love.

In the meantime, he was a man. His love for Tia didn't stop him from enjoying other women. It *did* stop him from committing to long-term relationships. No. He didn't walk that road. It wouldn't be fair. Not to the woman. Not to him.

So why were you making noises a little while ago about wanting to get to know her better? Why aren't you taking your cues from Rachael and ending this with "Well, it wasn't meant to be, nice knowing you, see you around sometime?"

Damned if he knew why.

Just like he didn't know why the thought of stripping her out of that prim and proper Royal Palms uniform and seeing her in nothing but that pretty, pale skin, had him instantly hard again and trying to figure out a way to make his little fantasy a reality. Or, at least, a way to make this moment last until he could work this puzzle out.

"Let me take you to dinner tonight," he said abruptly.

"No."

He laughed at her immediate and decisive reaction then reached for her hands, holding them loosely in his. "You didn't even think about it."

"I don't have to think about it. Look. You caught me off guard there, okay?" She pulled her hands free. Hiking herself down off the seawall, she tugged down her skirt and readjusted her blouse. "But that…" she paused searching for the words.

He decided to provide them for her. "That incredible, mind-bending, sexy-as-hell kiss that you enjoyed every bit as much as I did?" he said, reaching for her tie and helping her straighten it.

"Whatever." She batted his hands away as her face flushed red. "It was a mistake. I don't even know you." She held out her hand for her sunglasses then turned and walked toward the rented SUV.

"I was born Nathan Alejandro McGrory, second son of Gloria Sanchez McGrory and Ryan Nathaniel McGrory in Miami thirty-two years ago come July," he said, deciding he'd worry about the whys and the consequences later and followed her. "My brother's name is Antonio Nicholas McGrory. His wife's name is Tia. They've been married five years and have two beautiful children, Marco and Meredith."

When she glared at him over the roof of the SUV, he just grinned and unlocked the doors with the remote.

"I graduated from Ohio State, went to law school at Harvard. Joined the family shipping firm and worked as corporate council until five years ago when I established my own law firm—still in Miami. I have all my own teeth, I jog five miles a day and am as healthy as a horse. And if you can overlook the fact that I still sleep with my teddy bear, Ted, I'm a pretty regular guy."

Gotcha, he thought as a whisper of a grin tipped up one corner of her mouth.

"Now what else would you like to know?"

"I'd like to know," she said, rearranging her face back into a stern scowl as he pulled out into traffic, "what it's going to take to convince you I'm not interested."

He cast her a sideways glance as he headed for the Royal Palms, just three blocks down the street. "A reaction a hell of a lot cooler than the one I got when I kissed you."

Silence, as thick as syrup, filled the SUV as he pulled into the Royal Palms circular driveway and stopped under the portico.

"Goodbye, Mr. McGrory," she said and let herself out. "Thank you for lunch."

"I'll call you," he yelled as she jogged up the grand outer staircase toward the four sets of gleaming gold-and-plate-glass revolving doors.

"Don't bother," she tossed over her shoulder.

"No bother," he said to himself as she disappeared into the opulent hotel. He sat there for a long moment before he finally put the SUV in gear. And damn, if he wasn't grinning again. "No bother at all."

"Well?" Sylvie stood just inside the doorway to Rachael's office, drawing out the word in an attempt to interject any number of leading questions. The one she finally settled on was, "How was lunch?"

Rachael tossed her purse into her lower left desk drawer and dropped into her chair. She had to sit. Her knees were too weak to hold her another minute.

Oh, Lord. He'd scared her. Scared her good. He'd

gotten to her, and somehow she had to figure out a way to get herself back under control.

Angry with herself for letting things get out of hand between them, and with Sylvie for encouraging him, she propped her elbows on her desk, folded her hands in front of her and shot Sylvie an evil smile. "See if I cover for you the next time Edward from accounting comes looking for you. You remember Edward of the terminal dandruff and phlegmy cough? Edward of the little comb-over thingy he does with his ten oily strands of hair? Ever notice the way his eyes bug out when he hears your name?

"Oh, yeah, *Ms.* Sylvie." Rachael leaned back in her chair, linked her fingers together over her midriff and relished the horrified look on Sylvie's face. "Not only will I *not* cover for you, I will lead him to the end of the earth to find you. I will extol your virtues— or lack thereof—while we search, in such graphic detail the man will be drooling on his bowtie by the time we find you. And," she added, holding up a finger when Sylvie tried to cut her off, "I will, with great pleasure, relate to him how hot you are for his body—pudgy little paunch and all."

"All right. All right," Sylvie sputtered. "I get it. You're ticked. How was I supposed to know you'd lost your mind completely? How was I supposed to know you wouldn't want to go out with the most luscious hunk of mankind this woman has ever set eyes on?"

"Oh, I don't know," Rachael returned with mock confusion. "How *would* you have known? Maybe from hints the size of Mack trucks I was dropping about a fake appointment?"

Sylvie waved away her scowl with a sweep of a beautifully manicured hand. Her nails were crimson red today—with little white stars and stripes on the tips. "So sue me. I thought you were having a brain cramp. I mean, what woman in their right mind would not want to go out with that man?"

"This woman," Rachael insisted and told herself if she repeated it often enough, she'd begin to believe it.

"Which begs the obvious question—did you have a stroke or something?" Sylvie rose, leaned across the desk and touched her palm to Rachael's brow. "A fever, maybe?"

Rachael let out a deep breath and finally gave up a grudging smile. Sylvie meant well. "He's not my type, okay?"

Sylvie laughed. "Oh, sweetie. He is every woman's type."

"Yeah, well, I don't have time for every woman's type."

"You would, if you hadn't married yourself twenty-four seven to this job."

"I love this job," Rachael protested, pulling out her Palm Pilot and double-checking her afternoon appointments with the intention of grounding herself in her work.

"To the exclusion of having a life?" Sylvie asked, serious now as she met Rachael's eyes with kind concern.

"Why is it so hard for everyone to accept that I like my life exactly the way it is?"

"You are wasting away here, Rachael. You're

young. You're beautiful. You need to have someone special in your life.''

"I am not wasting away. I feed off this job. And Nate McGrory is not looking for someone special. He's looking for a fast, hot fling.''

"So…what's wrong with fast and hot just to get your juices going before they all dry up from lack of use? Let him rev your motor for a while. You don't have to fall in love with him. You just have to enjoy him.''

Sylvie's comments gave her pause. "This from a woman who was married for thirty-five years to the love of her life. *You* could do that? You could go for the sex and forget the rest?''

"We weren't talking about me. Buck and I—we were soul mates. We were like mallards. We mated for life. I have no interest in short, meaningless encounters.''

"And you honestly think I do?''

"No,'' Sylvie said soberly. "I don't. But who knows—maybe it would turn into something more. I saw the way he looked at you. He was really interested.''

"He was really interested in a conquest. It's not going to be me. Now—are we finished with this conversation or do I need to bring Edward back into the fray?''

Sylvie rose. "Okay, okay. Your life. Your call. The Davises are due in about five minutes,'' she added, letting the subject of Nate McGrory drop. "The file's on your desk.''

"Thanks,'' Rachael said and watched Sylvie walk toward the door. "Hey…I'm sorry I was taking my bad mood out on you. Thanks. Thanks for caring. It means a lot.''

''You always draw the line at caring,'' Sylvie groused, her voice trailing behind her as she left Rachael's office. ''I never get to meddle. I think I'd be really good at it.''

Rachael grinned and shook her head. ''Trust me on this—you *are* good at it.''

Sylvie was efficient, fun-loving and just a little on the quirky side. Rachael loved her. She could always count on Sylvie to get the job done, to make her laugh, and to take the time to ask, ''Are you all right?'' when she saw something in Rachael's eyes alerting her that no, she wasn't all right. On those rare occasions when Rachael actually let down her defenses enough to confide in her, Sylvie would take the time to listen and then gently ask her how long it had been since she'd talked with her mother.

Her gaze landed involuntarily on the framed family portrait sitting on her bookshelf—the family portrait she should have been a part of, but she had begged off, making excuses at the last minute, and told them to go ahead and have it taken without her.

She walked across her office, picked it up, rubbed her thumb across the smiling faces of her blond stepsisters. Allison and Carrie had been twelve and thirteen at the time the picture was taken four years ago. They were sweetly smiling, pretty in the yellow and pink sundresses she'd bought them for Christmas. Behind them, her hands resting with maternal love on their shoulders, Rachael's mother smiled her loving-wife-and-mother smile, while beside her, John, Rachael's stepfather, draped his arm over her mother's shoulders. The portrait of the perfect American family. Happy. Healthy. Complete.

She set the photograph back in its place. After all these years, it still surprised her to realize she wished she could be a part of that picture even though she was the one who had sabotaged it, as well as any meaningful relationship with her family. She shoved back the longing for something she purposefully denied herself then felt a pinch of relief when her phone rang. "Yes, Sylvie."

"You're mom's on line two."

Rachael's heart skipped a little beat. "Hi, Mom," she said brightly when she punched the button.

"Hey, kiddo. How's it going?"

"Good. Busy."

"Exactly why I called. I want to make sure you didn't forget about dinner Thursday."

Rachael groaned. She *had* forgotten. Sort of. "Oh, Mom. I'm sorry." She sank down on the corner of her desk as guilt flooded her. "I'm sorry," she repeated, reacting to her mom's disappointed silence. "I scheduled a late appointment—it's one I can't afford to miss. Can we reschedule?" she asked quickly, hoping to undo some of the damage.

"This *was* a reschedule," her mom reminded her. "I don't know, honey…sometimes I think you do this on purpose."

"You know that's not true." At least Rachael didn't think it was. "How about I call next week and we'll set something up?"

Her mother sighed heavily. "Sure, honey. Whatever works for you."

"I'll call, okay?"

"Okay."

Only they both knew she probably wouldn't call. She'd intend to…but she just wouldn't get around to it. Echoing her mother's goodbye, she pressed the end button on the receiver. Then she stared at the phone clutched loosely in her hand, wishing she could get past all the things that kept her from letting her mom be a part of her life.

"You canceled dinner again, didn't you?" Sylvie asked from her open doorway.

Rachael forced a smile and set the receiver in its cradle. Over a bottle of wine one night, she and Sylvie had had a little chat. At Sylvie's gentle probing, Rachael had told her about her childhood. Sylvie had nailed it in one.

"So you figure that since your dad was abusive to you and your mother, and since your mother eventually found someone who made her life complete, that *you* must have been the problem."

Well, yeah. Sylvie's astute assessment had pretty well summed up her inability to make any relationship work. Rachael knew it was a self-defense mechanism to push people away. She even understood, in a convoluted sort of way, why she did it. Could even justify that she was determined to have something a lot more stable in her life than love. Love was something elusive—something she'd never been able to count on, even from those people who professed they felt it for her.

Knowing *why* she pushed people away, however, didn't necessarily equate with figuring out how to do something about it without hurting them. So she generally avoided dealing with it at all. Now was no exception.

"I didn't cancel dinner. I just postponed. We'll reschedule soon."

Sylvie bit her tongue and nodded. "The Davises are here."

"Great," Rachael said, ignoring Sylvie's doubtful look. She forced a bright smile. "Give me a minute then send them in."

She needed a minute. A minute to remind herself that she was twenty-nine years old—not nine and clinging to her mother and wondering why her daddy hated her as they raced to the closest battered women's shelter to get away from another one of his blind, fist-swinging rages.

How many times had they run in the middle of the night—a dozen? twenty?—before her mother had finally gathered the courage to file for divorce and relocate from Ohio to Florida to get away from Calvin Matthews? It had been just the two of them then. Two against the world, her mother used to say as she kissed Rachael good night.

And then her mom had met John Cooper. He was the antithesis of Calvin Matthews. John was kind. He didn't drink. He treated her mother like a queen. He patted Rachael's head with absent affection. Everything was going to be wonderful. Everything was going to be great. And it was—until two years later, the year Rachael turned twelve and that first pretty little pink baby was born.

Like everyone else, Rachael loved Allison to distraction. "Don't hover," her mom used to scold.

''Don't always be loving on her. She needs some room. So do I.''

As it turned out, they all needed a lot of room from Rachael, who wanted so much to be a part of this beautiful new family that she annoyed them with her smothering attention.

It was gradual, the way they shut her out over the years. She was certain her mother wasn't even aware of what she and John had done to her—of how much it had hurt her always to feel that she was on the outside looking in. As if she was a part of her mother's past that reminded her of bad times. Even after her mother had confided several years ago that she'd suffered a deep depression after the girls were born, and even though intellectually Rachael had seen how that depression had affected her mom's treatment of her, she still felt the loss. She still pushed people away before they could push her.

A shrink would have a field day with her and a couch. Only she didn't need a shrink to tell her she had issues with commitment. Issues with trust. So what? She was doing just fine.

Sylvie thought Rachael should get involved with Nate McGrory? Not a chance. As she'd told him, she didn't do relationships, or more accurately, she ruined relationships by making sure no one ever got close enough to her to matter.

And that, she reminded herself, was why her position at the hotel suited her. She could calmly and with cool reserve plan weddings for people who walked in and then right back out of her life. They weren't looking for long term with her. They were looking for spectacular, short-term results. She gave them both. And she didn't get involved.

That was enough. She made it be enough.

The flowers started arriving from Nate the next day.

The note accompanying the roses on Tuesday said: Did I mention that big dogs and little children love me?

The note with the lilies on Wednesday read: Say the word and Ted is history.

"Ted?" Sylvie asked with a quirk of her brow.

"His teddy bear," Rachael supplied, fighting a grin and not liking herself much for giving in to it.

"You're not going to give me more than that are you?"

"Nope," she said, feeling smug, and went back to work.

"Oh, God, you're gonna love this one," Sylvie said the next day, laughing as she brought the latest exotic bouquet into Rachael's office and set it on her desk.

"I don't remember telling you that you could read my personal messages," Rachael groused as she snatched the card from Sylvie's outstretched hand. Her manufactured scowl faded when she read the card. She shook her head, rolled her eyes and finally grinned.

Me strong—like bull.

"Got to give the man credit. He's nothing if not persistent. And dogs and kids love him," Sylvie added with a grin. "And he's strong—like bull."

"Har har."

But it was Friday's offering that really dented her

defenses. No flowers this time. Just a hot and tasty
value meal from her favorite drive-in and a note that
read: There's a lot more where this came from.

"Are you just melting over there?" Sylvie asked
as she reached into the sack and dug out a cheese fry.

Oh yeah. She was melting. "No. I'm not melting.
I'm annoyed."

"My turn," Sylvie said. "Har har."

"Okay. So it's flattering. But I'm still annoyed.
And I'm really not interested."

Sylvie shook her head. "The man is willing to give
up his teddy bear for you," she reminded Rachael
with a waggle of her brows. "Trust me on this—
that's not a sacrifice to be taken lightly."

"I have two words for you," Rachael said sweetly,
folding her hands together on the top of her desk.
"Comb-over."

Sylvie hissed, made a cat's claw, then marched out
of the room.

Rachael grinned. And smelled the flowers. And ate
a fry. And told herself he could send all the flora and
junk food he wanted. She wasn't going to get involved with him. With him in Miami and her in West
Palm, she figured it was pretty much a sure bet she'd
seen the last of him anyway.

# Five

So much for sure bets, Rachael thought two weeks later. Not only had she *not* seen the last of Nate McGrory, she was seeing way too much of him—literally—as he sat a little to the right and way too close behind her watching Karen and Sam open gifts at their post-honeymoon party.

''From the looks of things, I'd say the honeymoon was a huge success,'' Nate whispered in her ear.

He was so close she could feel the warmth of his breath feather across her bare shoulder. His voice was hushed, as if he didn't want to take the focus away from the newlyweds—or as if he wanted to cocoon the two of them in an intimate little conversation.

Rachael reminded herself she didn't want to be intimate with Nate McGrory—conversationally or horizontally—so she did her darnedest not to react to the way he looked and smelled and smiled and the way he somehow managed to keep pressing his bare thigh against her leg. Or the way he'd lean over, just so, so that his broad chest grazed her bare shoulder. Or he'd arrange it so his fingers brushed hers as he passed her a glass of mimosa, or his breath would tickle the fine hair at her nape where she'd swept it up into a haphazard knot in deference to the heat.

More than once already this afternoon she was glad she'd worn her plain yellow cotton tank top and white capris instead of shorts to the casual gathering. More than once she'd wished she could make herself ignore him as she smiled across the great room at Sam and Karen. Just back from their honeymoon, they were glowing, tanned and rested and so completely in love it hurt, just a little, to watch them.

Along with Sam and Karen's immediate family, all members of the bridal party who could make it were gathered in the newlyweds' new home in Jupiter, just north of West Palm, while the happy couple opened their wedding gifts. They'd decided to make a party of it. At least thirty people were in attendance at the get-together that would wrap up with a backyard cookout then a game of volleyball, if the net set up near the pool was a clue. Rachael had been told to bring her swimsuit. She'd also been told Nate wasn't going make it.

So much for what she'd been told.

Rachael hadn't seen him since that day he'd shanghaied her into lunch then kissed her silly on the seawall. But he'd made sure she'd thought about him every day during the weeks since. And as often as she told herself to ignore him, she hadn't been able to get herself to reject the deliveries or throw the flowers in the trash, or toss the sinfully delicious burgers and fries. He hadn't called her though. She'd mulled that fact over with relief tinged just a little too heavily with regret and told herself to snap out of it.

Now he was here. And she couldn't get herself to stop thinking that he was even more dazzling and gorgeous than she'd remembered. And close. Lord, he was close.

His nylon shorts were short and black; his tank top was white. Both were stunning contrasts to the deep, natural tan of his skin. Both revealed an impressive amount of well-toned muscle and a soft pelt of dark chest hair. A tingling sensation streaked through her tummy at the thought of touching her fingers there— just there at the base of his throat—to experience its softness and the heat of the skin beneath.

"You smell great, by the way. Have I mentioned that?"

"Twice," she said grumpily and wished there wasn't something about his dogged persistence that made her want to get a little soft and mushy inside. People didn't go the extra mile for her. Men especially didn't. Her cold shoulder usually did the trick. But not with him.

He'd been lobbing little compliments her way all afternoon, making sure she couldn't ignore him if she tried.

She cast him a sideways glance, saw the heat in his laughing eyes and, tipping her mimosa to her lips, quickly looked away. Why did he have to seem so sweet in spite of his blatant flirting? And why did he have to look so good? He should look like a BuBu, sitting there with his legs spread wide, his elbows propped on his thighs, a delicate wineglass clasped loosely in his large hand. A Miami Dolphins baseball cap sat backwards on his head. His dark hair peeked out beneath the cap's bill in the back, touching his shoulders, looking silky soft and artfully styled instead of shaggy and unkempt.

She closed her eyes, mentally shook her head. He could have sat beside anyone, she thought as she edged a little to the left and away from him on the overstuffed hassock. Yet he had made a point of sitting by her—on a footstool that barely accommodated one, let alone two people.

"Can you play volleyball in those shoes?" he whispered, dropping his chin onto her bare shoulder and looking up at her from beneath a web of thick, dark lashes. She'd kill for lashes that thick. On most men they'd have looked effeminate. Since she'd already established he wasn't most men, it was a given that on him they looked darkly dangerous.

She jerked forward, breaking the contact. His look, his touch—both were too familiar and too loaded with sexual intent…and with the promise of fun and a silly kind of sweetness that she simply did not want to fall prey to.

She made a show of studying her three-inch platform sandals. "I can play volleyball in cowboy boots," she informed him silkily, "and still outplay you."

She wasn't sure what made her say it—she'd break her ankle if she didn't ditch the shoes before they started playing. Maybe it was the too, too easy way he had of turning her awareness meter up to overload.

Maybe it was the fact that he was so sure of himself—
and so determined to ignore every hint she'd dropped
that she wasn't interested and for him to just back off.

Maybe, it was because she was lying. She *was* interested, didn't want to be and he knew it.

"Oh-ho, baby." Unconcealed amusement shot
sparks through eyes the deep, rich brown of cappuc-
cino. "I think I detected a definite challenge in that
statement."

"No challenge," she said slowly, "just stating a
fact."

"Don't know how to break this to you, darlin'"
he whispered so the others couldn't hear him, "but
you're a little vertically challenged for the game. I'm
pretty certain your head won't even reach the bottom
of the net."

"Well, *darlin',*" she drawled back, latching on to
any reason to let her dander rise above this compul-
sion to like him and above the humming sexual
awareness for which she'd yet to find a defense,
"what I lack in height, I make up for in speed and
just plain meanness."

He covered his face with his hand then grinned at
her from between spread fingers. "Somehow I knew
a little mean streak would factor into any game you
decided was worth playing. I, for one, can't wait to
find out just how mean you can get."

She was pretty sure he was no longer talking about
volleyball. And, darn it, she was having a hard time
not grinning back. This was not good.

She forced starch into her spine. "You'd better
hope we're on the same team, McGrory."

He winked. "Any time you want to team up, *Matthews,* I'm more than ready for the merger."

"Uncle Nate!" a little voice cried in excitement from across the room.

Rachael looked up, glad for the distraction as approximately sixty pounds of squealing freckles and blond pigtails sporting a Popsicle-stained smile ran across the room and hurled herself into Nate's arms.

"Emily," he proclaimed, lifting her onto his lap and into a huge bear hug. He planted a smacking kiss on her cheek. "How's my favorite chuckle-head?"

"I'm seven now," the little cherub proclaimed, pride in her voice as she looped her hands around Nate's neck and grinned into his eyes with unbridled adoration.

"Seven? Already?" he asked, sounding properly astounded.

"Uh-huh. Pretty soon I'll catch up with you and we can get married, 'member?"

Nate hugged her hard and laughed. "I'm saving myself just for you, doll."

This silly little bit of banter elevated Emily's smile from proud to pleased.

And melted Rachael's heart.

*No fair.* Nate McGrory had to be gorgeous and sexy and rich and charming—and let's not forget strong—like bull—but did he have to be sweet and gentle and indulgent with children, too? *Big dogs and little children loved him.* Rachael dropped her forehead to her hand and wondered if he helped little old ladies across the street.

"I'll be just as pretty as Karen won't I?" Emily asked, her eyes full of hope.

"Every bit, sweetie. Do you know my friend, Rachael?"

Perfect. Now he was going to draw her into the conversation with this adorable little imp and make her like him even more.

"Hi, Emily."

Emily smiled then looked her up and down. "Don't you think Uncle Nate is handsome?"

"Um…well—"

"Sure she does," Nate supplied, grinning over the top of Emily's tow head. "She's just a little shy about saying what she thinks. Isn't that right, Rachael?"

She forced a tight smile for Emily. "Yeah. Shy. That's me."

"He's not really my uncle," Emily explained. "He's Uncle Sam's friend so I call him Uncle Nate 'cause he's like one of the family. Hey—wanna go swimmin'?" she asked Nate, skipping on to bigger and better things with a mercurial shift of topics that left Rachael's head spinning.

"Sure," Nate said. "*Wanna* go with us?" he asked Rachael, the dare evident in his devil grin.

Just as she was about to launch into an emphatic no thanks, grateful for the opportunity to place some much-needed distance between herself and Mr. Perfectly Wonderful, Emily joined in on the arm-twisting.

"Come on Rachael. It'll be fun."

"Yeah," Nate said, covertly raking her body with a gaze as hot and smoky as his voice, "It'll be fun."

"Let's go get our suits on." Emily slipped off Nate's lap and latched on to Rachael's hand. "I've got a bikini—a red one. What have you got?"

What did she have? Nate's silent but obvious interest in Rachael's suit made it clear that what she had was trouble—with a capital *T* and that rhymed with *P* and that stood for pool—and not the kind Meredith Willson had in mind when he'd written his famous song from the *Music Man*.

"Hurry up, silly," Emily insisted, tugging her to her feet, "or Nate will beat us to the water."

"Last one in's got to pay with a kiss," Nate said, eyebrows waggling. His soft chuckle trailed behind her when Rachael practically dragged Emily toward the cabana at a dead run.

At ten that night, Rachael glanced across the front seat of her car to where Nate sat holding an ice bag on his right eye. She let out a deep breath, braked for a red light and flipped her left-turn signal.

She hadn't meant to bloody his lip. She even felt a little bad about the way his right eye was swollen. She'd only wanted to prove a point. Well, okay. She'd wanted to do more than that. As she'd faced him across the volleyball net after their swim, her team down five zip with the spike king, McGrory, scoring four of the points, she'd wanted to beat the pretty-boy smile right off his poster-boy face. She'd wanted to put him in his place and when his ego collapsed like the portable lawn chair she'd stowed in her trunk along with her empty salad bowl before heading home, she'd wanted to watch him slink away with his tail tucked so securely between his legs there'd be no chance he'd ever call her again.

So far, it was a dud of a plan.

Why? Well, it was mostly because aside from his

blatant interest in her, Rachael had seen a side of him tonight that Karen had been telling her about and that she hadn't wanted to believe. He'd let up on her the moment he'd slipped into the pool—all caramel-gold skin and hard, rippling muscle. He'd extracted a peck on the cheek from Emily who had made it a point to be the last one in. Then he'd pretty much left Rachael alone to drool in peace while he'd repeatedly lifted Emily up onto his shoulders so she could dive off, or coach her when she jumped off the diving board, or show her the nuances of the back stroke.

He'd been gentle, patient, and full of fun with the little girl—and a regular Boy Scout with her. He'd taken a long, hard, appreciative look at her in her modest black one-piece, honed in on what could only have been distress plastered across her face and must have decided he'd stroke out if he so much as came near her, water dripping from that glorious black hair and trailing down his very buff body. So, he'd kept his distance.

Just when she'd thought she could dislike him for using a little girl to get to her, he turned into a gentleman. Just her luck, Nate McGrory drew lines and didn't cross them. How did you defend against those kind of underhanded tactics? He really was more than he appeared to be. A genuine nice guy. A guy she could lose her head over…and *that* was the reason she couldn't let anything happen between them.

Was she the only person on the planet who saw disaster written all over this?

It didn't matter that he was as nice as everyone said he was—like Karen who marveled that unlike most filthy-rich men, he wasn't quirky, or cruel or self-absorbed. He was *normal*. From Rachael's experience, he was an anomaly among the rich and famous—and he wasn't supposed to be, darn it. He was supposed to be severely flawed in the character department and he had the nerve to be well-adjusted, kind, charming, patient, sexy and…yada yada yada.

And *that* brought her to the real reason she'd lost it on the volleyball court. It had been hit him or hug him and, well…she really did have a little mean streak in her. Unfortunately, it had come out with a vengeance and he'd paid the price. Gracefully, she might add—damn him.

"How's the eye?" she asked as guilt got the best of her. Just as it had gotten the upper hand when she'd grudgingly agreed that since she'd maimed him—his words—the very least she could do was give him a ride to his hotel since he wasn't in any shape to drive—again, his words and his assessment. She'd figured he could drive just fine. No one else had.

Fine, she thought grumpily. She'd knuckled under. She was giving him a ride.

Much of this was Kimmie's fault, she thought in disgust as she eased into the right lane. Kimmie's and Karen's and Sam's who had all been on her team. Kim had been bemoaning a broken nail for the better part of the first set. Sam and Karen spent more time fabricating reasons to run into each other and indulge in long hot kisses than keeping their heads on the game. Her natural competitive spirit had kicked into overdrive. *Somebody* had to do something to stop the one-man wrecking crew. Rachael had felt obligated to step up to the plate. Or, in this case, up to the net.

And had proceeded to drill the ball straight into his face.

"I'll live," he said and when she glanced at him, she saw that incorrigible smile curve his lips. "I'd rather talk about how you can make it up to me."

The suggestion in his tone left little doubt that his idea of making it up to him involved the two of them naked somewhere kissing more than boo-boos. After seeing him in his swim trunks today, she had less to imagine and more to anticipate in that area. "I said I was sorry."

"But was your heart in it?"

Oh, God. He was going to make her smile again if she wasn't careful. "My heart was in the spike I slammed into your face. But my good intentions were behind my apology if that's any consolation."

"Fair enough. Just so you understand that *my* good intentions must have lost out if my attorney hits you with a lawsuit."

Her head swiveled toward him. "You're kidding."

"Probably." He slumped deeper into the seat, his long legs cramped against the consol of her compact car. The muscles in his thighs were lax, his head lolled against the headrest as he pretended to consider. "I'm not sure yet. Maybe we could litigate this ourselves. Say…over a nice bottle of merlot and a candle-light dinner tomorrow night?"

The look on his face was both endearing and maddening. Darn him, he just wouldn't let up. "I don't get you, McGrory," she groused aloud. "Besides the fact that I'm clearly not interested, I don't run in your social or financial circles. We probably have nothing in common. So why are you bothering?"

"Why does the sun rise?" he returned, playfully mimicking her dramatic tone.

She rolled her eyes.

He laughed, but the sound was colored with frustration as he resettled the ice pack on his eye. "Okay. Try this. Instead of wondering why, why, why, let's go with why *not?* Why not just go with it and see where it leads? Why are you making this so difficult? Why can't you just give it up, go out with me and see if we enjoy each other's company as much as every red blood cell in my body is telling me we will?"

Well, he didn't much mince words did he? It didn't help that her blood cells were doing some talking, too. It was her job to lie for them. "I don't want to sleep with you."

He snorted. "Now tell me you're sorry you broke my face. I'll try to believe that, too."

"Okay. I *might* want to sleep with you," she finally confessed, then could have kicked herself when he sat up, threw an arm over the seat back, lowered the ice pack and shot her a victorious smile.

*Had she really said that?*

"Progress at last."

"But that's biology," she defended hastily. "Simple chemistry."

"Two of my favorite subjects."

She sighed deeply. "I don't do casual sex, Nate."

"Who said anything about casual?"

His voice was soft, sincere and too much to believe. So she didn't. "Isn't that what this is about?"

He was quiet for a moment before saying, "Don't you think you're selling us both short?"

She couldn't think of a single thing to say to that.

"How about I tell you what this is about," he continued as if he were actually giving it some serious thought. "It's about this attraction and this general feeling that if we walk away from each other without ever seeing what direction this takes, we're both going to be very, very sorry.

"Come on, Rachael. Don't you ever just free fall?" he asked when she remained stubbornly silent.

It was more than disconcerting to admit her silence was mainly because she was simply running out of arguments, or at least running out of strength to defend against his.

"Don't you ever just risk something and screw the consequences?"

Finally, an easy question. "No. Never," she said. It was the risk factor of the equation that finally got her back on track. She didn't do risk. She did safe and secure. She needed safe and secure. He was neither of those things.

"Then don't you think it's time you considered it?"

Rather than answer, she evaded. She seemed to do that a lot around him.

"I believe this is your hotel," she said, pulling up in front of the charming and pricey Brazilian Court. Very intentionally, she left her foot on the brake and the car in gear as a valet magically appeared and opened the passenger-side door. It took everything in her to stare straight ahead instead of meeting Nate's eyes.

"I don't suppose a last-ditch plea for mercy would

convince you to come up to my room and administer a little triage?''

Her snort said, Not on your life, although she had to wrap her fingers around the steering wheel and hang on tight.

''Didn't think so.''

Silence filled her car then, as intrusive as a floodlight.

''If I give you my number, you won't call me, will you?'' he asked as if he already knew the answer.

She shook her head, resolute in the face of the genuine regret she heard in his voice.

This was it then. He finally understood. A disappointment she hadn't expected colored her words as well. ''No. I won't call.''

Another long moment passed before he finally got out of the car then ducked back down so he could see inside. ''Then I'll call you.''

She jerked her head toward him. ''Nate—''

He stopped her protest with a shake of his head. ''I'll call you, Rachael.'' Then he turned and, tossing the ice pack from hand to hand, walked into the hotel.

Rachael was fitting the key into the lock of her town house door when her phone rang fifteen minutes later.

''Just wanted you to know I make good on my promises,'' Nate said without preamble when she snatched up the receiver and breathed a breathless hello.

She sank down on her sofa, too aware of her pleasure at hearing his voice. For once, she didn't fight the involuntary reaction to smile. "A man of his word."

"I think I might have covered that in one of the cards I sent with the flowers."

Still smiling, she laid her head back against the sofa. "So you did."

"Did I mention I was persistent, too?"

She touched her fingers to her curving lips. "Among other things, I believe so, yes."

Silence settled like a silk scarf all light and shimmery and set all of her senses on simmer mode. She stared into the darkness of her living room, her heart pounding, afraid she was waiting for him to ask her out again, afraid she'd say yes if he did.

"Good night, Rachael."

"Good night," she whispered after the moment it took her to process the finality of his words—and to convince herself she wasn't disappointed that he'd given up. "Take care of that eye."

He chuckled. "I'll do that."

And then he hung up.

Rachael sat in the dark for several minutes, thinking about all those things she'd promised herself she wouldn't think about. Like how, under all that arrogance, she was beginning to believe that those who knew him best were right when they swore he was a kind and generous man. How he made her laugh, even when she didn't want to. How her entire body had come alive in a way that had elevated her to a new height of awareness the moment their eyes connected.

She thought of how long it had been since any man had drawn this strong a reaction from her. Of how long it had been since she'd let down her guard enough to want to react this way. And finally, she silently confessed to how badly she wanted to be with Nate McGrory.

With a low growl of frustration, she rose, threw her deadbolt and headed for the shower.

She was applying the cream rinse to her hair before she realized she'd been humming an old show tune under her breath.

If only she could wash that man out of her life as easily as she rinsed her shampoo out of her hair.

# Six

Sunday dinner at the McGrory Miami mansion was always part business, part family catch-up session and pure torture for Nate. Not that anyone would ever know. He always made sure they didn't.

In the corner of the lanai, under the shade of a coconut palm, Nate's father, Ryan, and his brother, Tony, huddled over the chessboard talking shipping business and baseball and grumbling good-naturedly at each other over their offensive and defensive strategies. Nate was several yards away in the yard, playing catch with little Marco, Tony and Tia's four-year-old while Meredith, their two-year-old, napped in the nursery.

Regardless of the full-time household staff at the elaborate estate his father laughingly referred to as Dublin West, his mother, Gloria, who Nate resembled physically, sharing her dark hair and complexion and eyes, insisted on preparing the family's Sunday dinner. With dinner over, she was in the kitchen putting the finishing touches on some sinfully sweet desert. Eventually, she'd carry it out to the lanai and insist they all eat it, regardless of the fact that they were still stuffed to the gills from a dinner that somehow managed to blend Cuban and Irish cuisine into a sumptuous feast.

"We don't see much of you anymore, Nate. The kids miss you. So does Tony. So do I."

Nate gathered himself, managed a smile then glanced over his shoulder and into the eyes of the woman he'd loved and lost to his brother. Tia. Beautiful, sensitive, gentle Tia. Seeing her at these Sunday gatherings always brought home the bittersweet reminder that he loved her. But since Tony was the one who'd been smart enough to admit it and then do something about it, that had left Nate in the cold. To date, he hadn't found a way to combat his love for her save stow it away.

"You know how it goes, sis. Too much work, too little time."

And it was just too hard to be around them together. No one knew that he loved her, of course. Nate had never professed his feelings; he'd never hurt Tony or Tia that way. They'd been friends forever, the three of them, and then one day, out of the blue, Tony announced he and Tia were getting married. Nate had been stunned—and a little confused. All he could think was, Man…how could I have been so blind? Not just to Tony and Tia's love for each other, but to his feelings for Tia.

It wasn't a conclusion he'd reached overnight, but after a while, when no woman ever measured up, he'd finally realized it was his love for Tia that kept him from committing to a relationship. Most of the women he saw didn't seem real next to her. They were pampered, plastic princesses; they wanted him for his wealth, his reputation, his social status.

It had finally come to him then, that he'd missed his opportunity for a soul mate. But, he'd carried on. He'd just gone about his business of enjoying life as best as he could. Some things, however, were just too tough. Like seeing Tia and Tony together on a daily basis. That's the reason he'd opted out of the family business shortly after they'd gotten married even though he'd told the old man he simply needed to be out on his own. That had been five years ago.

And then came Rachael Matthews…and she had him buzzed on something that had eluded him for a very long time. Fascination.

"What's this I hear about a new woman in your life?" Tia asked, rousing him from his musings.

Nate caught the ball when Marco tossed it then pasted on another brotherly smile. Tia's brown eyes were big and round, her full mouth smiling and curious. "Tony has a big mouth and you know I never kiss and tell."

Speaking of kisses, he'd spent a lot of time thinking about the hot kiss he'd shared with Rachael, even now he felt an answering heat pool low in his gut. Interesting. He'd never so much as kissed Tia. Never made any attempt to relay his feelings. Marriage was sacred. So was his brother's love. And while he'd come to believe there wasn't another woman out there for him, he'd grown up in this lovingly blended Latino and Irish family and he wanted very badly to believe in the continued solvency of the institution of marriage.

Not that he thought it would ever happen for him. Not now. And he hated that. Really hated it—more so every day. Once he'd wanted home, hearth, kids—the whole nine yards. He'd given up on that scenario because the one woman he saw completing the picture was out of reach.

So why did you mention Rachael to Tony, a little voice in his head asked.

Darned if he knew. He saw a lot of women. Enjoyed the hell out of them as long as they understood up front it was fun and games and nothing more. But he never talked about them to his family.

Back to square one. Why Rachael? Most women fawned over him. Rachael wouldn't give him the time of day. It tickled the hell out of him that she wasn't impressed by his money or his looks or his social status. She was smart and feisty and dedicated and driven—all things that had been said about him at one time or another.

Bottom line, she intrigued him, but he'd never let things get too serious between them. It wouldn't be fair. Not to her. Not when his heart was lost to Tia.

You told her your interest wasn't casual, bozo.

Yeah. There was that. Was he resorting to lying now to get a woman into bed with him? If so, why? Was it the challenge? Or was he getting tired of fun and games and looking, again, for something he'd given up on having?

"Hello-o-o."

He jerked his head around. Curiosity tinged with amusement colored Tia's face.

"Where'd you go, Nate?"

He'd totally zoned out on her. "Sorry. I was concentrating on my main man here," he lied with a grin and tossed the ball to Marco. He laughed when the little boy made a dramatic dive to catch it, bobbled it, then belly-crawled across the grass to retrieve it.

"Come, come," Nate's mother called from the lanai. "Dessert is ready."

"That's our cue, boyo." Relieved for the opportunity to escape the one-on-one conversation with Tia, Nate scooped Marco up and onto his shoulders and dodging a pineapple palm, headed for the lanai.

Then he spent the rest of the afternoon wondering why was working so hard to breach Rachael Matthews's—of the saucy green eyes and irresistible mouth—defenses.

Two weeks after Karen and Sam's party, Rachael had decided Nate McGrory had finally gotten the message. Oh, he'd called a few times but Sylvie had deflected him for her. And then the calls had stopped altogether. She hadn't seen so much as a daisy or smelled a rose with some silly note attached since. And that was good. That was…great, she told herself as she sat at her desk looking over an array of printed material on entrées and wine selections for the upcoming Jenson wedding reception.

"And it only took a blackened eye and a bloodied lip to do the job," she muttered under her breath.

A sound at her open door brought her head

up…and set her heart racing as she connected with the vivid cappuccino-brown of Nate McGrory's eyes.

While her heart did a back flip and shot heat to every extremity in her body, his only reaction was that one corner of his fabulous mouth kicked up in an endearingly boyish smile.

"The door was open," he offered by way of apology for interrupting her.

"I…um…"

His smile widened. "No life guard on duty today?"

"Excuse me?"

"Your assistant? She's not running interference today?"

"Oh." He was referring to Sylvie who had been reluctantly screening her calls—several of which had been from Nate. All of which Rachael had made up some excuse not to take until he'd finally stopped calling. "She must have…I don't know. She must be running an errand or something."

"My good luck."

She could only stare as he shoved his hands deep into his trouser pockets and leaned a shoulder against the doorframe.

When her phone rang, she couldn't help but think *Saved by the bell.*

She dealt with the call, all the while watching him while he prowled around the room, checking out her view, as well as the personal marks she'd put on her office.

"Your older sister?" he asked looking over his shoulder when she disconnected. He held the picture of her mother and stepfather and stepsisters in his hand.

Unable to stop herself, she walked around her desk and lifted the portrait from his hands. "Mother," she said stiffly.

She read the questions in his eyes, but set the photograph back on the shelf before he could voice them. He took the hint and let it go.

"So, how's it going, Rachael?"

It had been two weeks since she'd left him at the Brazilian Court with a promise that she wouldn't call. She'd thought of him every day—and night—since. Sitting close beside her on that tiny hassock. Tanned, wet skin in the pool. Rippling muscles spiking a volleyball. Irreverent grin and bedroom-brown eyes.

*That's* how it was going.

She walked back to her desk and sank into her chair before her knees buckled because he was standing here in the flesh with that delicious face and that amazing smile and extraordinary body.

*That's* how it was going.

And she thought of his gentleness with Emily and his friendship with a good man like Sam and the resigned disappointment in his eyes when she'd said, no, she wouldn't call.

*That's* how it was going.

"Busy," she said and left it at that.

"Ah. So that would explain why you couldn't take my calls."

She blinked, folded her hands together on top of her desk and ordered herself to tough it out. "If it makes you feel better to think so."

He laughed. "Don't you want to know what brings me to Palm Beach?"

She rose, gathered the literature together and

tapped it on her desk to straighten it. "My guess would be business, since there's nothing else here for you."

He stabbed an imaginary knife in his chest and sagged against the doorjamb. "You have a mean heart, Rachael Matthews."

She crossed the room, opened a cabinet and tucked the material neatly inside the Jenson file, praying he wouldn't see her hands shaking—or her heart beating beneath her blouse. "I thought we'd already established that."

"Why yes, my eye's fine. Thanks for asking," he said brightly and settled a hip on the corner of her desk.

She threw him what she hoped passed for a bland look as she returned to her desk and sat behind it.

"Okay, here's the deal," he began without preamble. "I've been thinking and this is the way I've got it figured. I've been too subtle with you."

She leaned back in her chair, regarded him with an incredulous stare. Then, because he was just so impossible, she laughed. "You don't have a subtle bone in your body."

"The flowers, the phone calls," he went on, ignoring her disbelieving look, "they just don't cut it with a woman like you. I need to be more decisive. I need to be more assertive."

"Nate," she began, but he cut her off.

"So I've made reservations at Mara Lago for tonight."

Had he said Mara Lago?

Rachael had *always* wanted to see Mara Lago, but like so many things in her life, the idea of ever setting foot inside the palatial private club was beyond her. Mara Lago was the famous Post mansion on South Ocean Boulevard that Donald Trump had purchased and transformed into an exclusive members-only club. Only the obscenely rich could afford membership. She catered to the obscenely rich; she did not rub elbows with them.

She studied Nate McGrory's face, let her gaze slip down to the white silk shirt that she recognized as Armani, to the butter-soft loafers that were most likely Gucci or Prada. They were designer names she knew, styles she admired but could rarely afford. She'd known he was rich but Mara Lago wasn't just rich. It was mega rich and it elevated their differences to heights too lofty to comprehend.

"Mara Lago?" she repeated, unable to mask the wistfulness as his smile broadened in victory.

"Yep." He crossed his arms over his chest and settled in to enjoy her discomfort. "I decided it was time to roll out the big guns."

"So...I'm supposed to be impressed?"

"If that's what it takes to get you to say yes.

"Look," he added when she just stared at him, "I figure it this way. Something or someone in the past has hurt you and I'm paying the price. That doesn't strike me as fair."

"Fair?" she repeated, blindsided by his assumption. Dumbstruck by his accuracy.

"Good. You agree."

"What did I agree to?"

"Seven o'clock, I'll send a limo."

And with that, he rose and walked out the door.

When Sylvie poked her head into Rachael's office

five minutes later, she was still staring into space and floating in a fog, wondering what barge had just hit her.

Rachael slid a glance toward her bedside clock and groaned. Six fifty-five. The limo would be pulling up in front of her town house any minute. For the hundredth time, she considered changing her mind. She hadn't told Nate she'd go, after all. But we were talking Mara Lago here. *Mara Lago.*

It wasn't that she had any wish to elevate her social status by being seen with the elitist crowd who frequented Mara Lago or any of the other exclusive clubs for which Palm Beach was famous. She had no illusions about who she was and where she belonged—which was definitely not in the hub of Palm Beach society where women like Gweneth Buckley called the shots and basically ran the show with their formal balls and charity functions that kept the cash flowing and the economy pumped.

No, she didn't want to be a part of that. But Mara Lago held a mystical appeal to her. She'd read stories about the Post empire, about the parties they'd thrown, the grandeur of the estate and it had always been her dream to just once…

Kimmie, she thought, eyes narrowed, as understanding dawned. Kim knew about her Mara Lago fantasy and even though Rachael had made her promise not to talk to Nate about her, it was obvious she'd spilled her guts. No doubt she and Nate had been talking again and she'd relayed that little tidbit of information. And, of course, he'd capitalized on it.

That did it. She'd been manipulated. And this night wasn't going to happen.

"But we're talking Mara Lago," she reminded herself with a groan, and, damn her weak-willed hide, she started reconsidering again. She'd already done her makeup and her hair, after all. And she was dressed for the occasion—or was she?

Because she often played MC or hostess for wedding receptions held at the Royal Palms, she was given a generous clothing allowance. The proof was in the discarded pile of cocktail dresses she'd slipped in and out of then tossed in a heap on her bed. She'd once thought of them as sophisticated and tasteful. Tonight, they simply seemed sedate. And boring. Not so, the dress she was currently wearing.

She glared at her reflection in the mirror, assessing the siren-red, sequined Spandex tube dress. It was so not her. Kimmie had talked her into buying it in a weak moment. She'd never had the nerve to wear it. It revealed way too much leg, way too much chest and sent a definitive statement to any man with half a clue: I wore this so you could peel it off me.

What was she thinking?

She was about to shimmy out of the skin-tight dress that only allowed for a thong underneath it when her buzzer rang.

Her heart fluttered. With a steadying breath, she stalked out to the foyer and pressed the call button— her mind changed *again*—and prepared to send what was undoubtedly Nate's limo driver on his way. "Yes."

"Ms. Matthews?"

"Yes."

"Mr. McGrory bid me to extend his wishes for a good evening and to inform you his car is at your disposal to take you to Mara Lago at your convenience."

"Thank you," she said and bit the proverbial bullet. "I'll be down in a few minutes."

She drew a deep breath, squared her shoulders and went in search of her silver heels. She was going to do this. She was going to let Nate have his way and meet him tonight.

But, she decided, a sudden burst of resolve rolling through her, she was going to make him pay for manipulating her this way. He wanted to play games? Fine. Let 'em begin. At this point, she didn't even care who won or what was at stake. She just wanted him to know she could hold her own and tonight she was going to prove it.

He wanted assertive? He was getting it. In spades. In her line of work, she'd finessed more business and massaged more decisions than anyone would ever imagine. It came with the territory. Give the customer what they wanted—only make sure you sold them on the idea of wanting it in the first place—and everybody went home happy.

Nate McGrory thought he wanted her? Well, he was going to get her—until she said enough was enough. She wasn't a siren by nature. She wasn't a tease. But she could manipulate with the best of them if she had to. And she'd had a bellyful of Nate McGrory's tactics. It was time to pull a few tricks out of her own bag.

Oh yeah, she thought, applying a shimmering crimson gloss to her lips, the red dress was the perfect choice after all.

She dabbed perfume—heavy on musk and blatantly sensual—behind her ears, between her breasts, on the pulse points at her wrists, then adjusted the top of her sequined dress downward to show a little more cleavage. Satisfied with the results, she snagged her little beaded bag from her dresser and headed for the door.

And what, exactly, do you think you're accomplishing with this little act, asked the devil on her shoulder.

Satisfaction, that's what. She hadn't started this, he had. She hadn't wanted it, but he'd pressed. Well, she was going to press back. If Nate McGrory wasn't drooling and reduced to monosyllabic mutterings by the time she was through with him tonight, she'd go out and join a nunnery.

By seven, Nate was afraid he'd blown it. Pushed Rachael too hard and driven her further away. Lord knew, she had a stubborn streak as long as the Florida coastline and he—well, he'd been heavy-handed and blatantly obnoxious, not to mention pretty damned presumptuous.

Eyes on the Moroccan-style gated drive guarding Mara Lago from the general public, he watched for the limo and reviewed his list of transgressions. First, he'd assumed she didn't have plans for tonight. Second, he'd counted on her shock at his unexpected appearance in her office to stall her resistance. And third, he'd relied heavily on Mara Lago as his ace in the hole. Bless Kim for the inside info.

"And thank you Lady Luck for sitting on my

shoulder tonight,'' he murmured in a sigh of relief as the hired limo eased through the gates and pulled up in front of the Mara Lago Club at approximately seven-ten.

He was feeling pretty good now, cocky as all get out as he shot his cuffs, smoothed the lapels on his tux and walked down the steps. He waited as the chauffeur rounded the limo and opened the rear passenger door.

And then he got a look at her—and damn near felt his tongue hit the ground.

''Well...hello,'' he said huskily as he took the hand she offered and steadied her as she stepped out of the stretch.

She looked *incredible*.

All creamy skin—lots of it—and slim toned limbs that looked a mile long in those silver stiletto heels that sent a jolt of electricity straight to his groin. She looked chic and elegant. Beyond pretty to gorgeous. And hot. The lady was definitely hot. Her sexy little tush was barely covered by her short, short dress. And her breasts—full and high and lush—all but spilled out of the red sequined bodice.

It wasn't as if he wasn't used to the company of blatantly sexy and obviously interested women, but on Rachael—the original power-suit and power-broker type—the deviation from the norm was...well...it brought out the animal in him.

And if he didn't get the beast leashed, he was going to tumble her right back into the limo and start working that miniscule little red number down her luscious curves in about another second. He was about to suggest just that when he caught her eye.

A victorious gleam—one he'd never seen before—sparkled in her mystic green eyes. And just that fast, he knew.

She was messing with him. Big-time.

Damn. He pulled her into his arms. Laughing through a groan, he tipped her face up to his with a curled index finger under her chin. "You cunning little witch. You're trying to kill me here, aren't you?"

She smiled serenely. "*Kill* might be a little excessive, not to mention illegal."

"Torture then?"

"That'll work."

He laughed again, then growled as he lowered his mouth to within an inch of hers. "How about we skip dinner and go directly to the nearest bed before I do something illegal right here in the driveway?"

She evaded his lips, regarded him with pity. "I hate to break it to you, sport, but you're not the main attraction here."

"Mara Lago," he deduced with a sage nod and knew he'd been taken to task by a master. "Hoist with my own petard."

"Oh, would you listen to that. He's not only well-heeled, he has a brain in that pretty little head." She patted his cheek and smiled as though her pet puppy had just performed a new trick. "What more could a girl ask for?"

Brushing a kiss across his lips, she pulled out of his embrace, her hands lingering on the lapels of his tux before she slowly turned and strolled toward the grand entrance doors.

"I'm a dead man," Nate muttered with a shake of his head as he watched the sassy sway of her hips.

"I'd say so, yes, sir," the chauffeur agreed from behind him.

Nate turned and threw him a grin. "But what a way to go, huh?"

"What a way indeed," the man said with a tip of his hand to his hat.

"Coming, Nathan?" the little vixen had the nerve to ask as she waited for him at the door.

"Oh, yes, ma'am," he said on a grimace. "One way or the other, with or without you, I'm definitely coming tonight."

"Tell me something," Nate said later as they stood barefoot in the sand while the rush of the surf sluiced around them and moonlight washed across her face, limning her delicate features in gold.

"You're wondering what I'm wearing beneath this dress, right?" She blinked up at him, all guileless eyes and shimmering red lips.

"Well, there is that," he agreed with a grin. He'd been wondering all night, in fact. He was pretty sure he had it figured out—there was little between her and him but a foot or two of moonlight and what the eye could see. Quickly steering his rogue thoughts away from dangerous territory, he took her hand and led her down the beach toward the jetty. "But actually, I was thinking of something else."

He'd peeled off his shoes and socks at the base of the wooden steps and left them there in the sand along with her strappy silver heels. Parked above and behind them on the street behind the seawall, the limo and driver waited in discreet silence.

Nate hadn't meant for them to end up on the beach

when they'd left Mara Lago. But he hadn't been ready to take her home. Just as he hadn't been ready to do what he'd decided he had to do when he took her there.

He'd have to leave her. It was the only way he could convince her he was in this a little deeper than he'd ever been in a relationship before—that this wasn't just a game of chase and conquest. He still hadn't figured out exactly what game he *was* playing—or even if it was a game anymore—but in the meantime, she was killing him by degrees in that glittering skin of a dress, with her irreverent little smiles and staged-to-be-wicked innuendos.

Oh yeah. She had his number. And she was giving back as good as he'd given her. With one exception. It had been apparent from the beginning that she'd set out to teach him a lesson tonight then leave him twisting in the wind.

It was time to eat some humble pie.

"Rachael…is there even a remote chance that we can start all over?"

She stopped walking when he did then looked up at him. "Start *what* all over?"

"Oh, how about everything?" He smiled, shook his head. "I've been a jerk."

She regarded him with an interest that showed he'd surprised her. "You finally picked up on that, did you?"

He grunted and let her soft smile take some of the sting out of her agreement. "Yeah, well, never let it be said I don't recognize some of my own tactics when I see them thrown back at me. I've learned my lesson."

She batted her eyes, all guileless innocence. "And what lesson might that be?"

"The one where I finally realize I've been coming on to you like a sailor hitting the beach after a year without shore leave. I've been in your face, obnoxious, intrusive—umm—don't hesitate to jump in here any time and stop me," he suggested with a little plea for mercy.

She thought about it then shook her head. "I don't think so. I'm enjoying this little bit of soul-searching far too much."

"Just like you enjoyed putting me in my place tonight."

"I did do that, didn't I?"

"Oh yeah. You've got me revved up, wrung out and singed to the bone—and you don't have any intention of letting me past your apartment door, do you?"

"Got it in one, *sailor*."

He tipped his head back, grinned up at the sky, then down at her. He took her hands in his, watched the play of his thumbs as he rubbed them along her knuckles. "Let's try this. Hi," he said softly, "I'm Nate. Nate McGrory. I saw you at Karen and Sam's wedding. Haven't stopped thinking about you since. And I'd really, really like to get to know you."

Oh, damn, Rachael thought morosely as she looked into his eyes. Why the heck did he have to go and get sweet on her when she'd had him exactly where she'd wanted him? Why couldn't he just have continued playing this Sex-and-the-City game they'd been playing all night long so she could leave him at her door and congratulate herself for a job well done?

His eyes were so dark, so sincere, and truly apologetic. And it just…melted her.

Warning bells clanged in every corner of her brain. She told herself to run, not walk, back across the beach, up the steps, hail a cab and get as far away from this man as fast as she could. And yet she stood there.

With that one look, those few words, he'd managed to win the fight she'd been waging against succumbing to his wit, his charm, yes, even his arrogance and steamroller tactics.

She'd set out to show him tonight—with wicked smiles and teasing innuendos—that two could play this game, but that she could make her own rules. Rule number one: Bring him to his knees. Rule number two: Leave him frustrated and fixated and finally understanding she didn't have to play his game if she didn't want to. Rule number three: Tell him goodbye.

For three years she'd distanced herself from the pressure of this kind of involvement with her absorption in her work and with a steely resolve not to open herself up to the one thing she knew would always elude her. And yet she stood there. Just stood there, looking down at their joined hands, then up into his eyes.

"Hi," she whispered, and Lord help her, in one insane, irrational moment, blew every defense she'd worked so hard to erect and stepped headlong into certain heartbreak. "I'm Rachael. And I think maybe I'd like to get to know you, too."

# Seven

"Again? Tonight?" Sylvie asked with an intrigued arch of her brow as she settled into a chair opposite Rachael's desk. She began working on her nails with an emery board. "That's what? Three times this week?"

"Twice," Rachael corrected her. "And I didn't know you were counting."

"Sweetie—I can count my heartbeats every time that man calls, or every time he and his killer smile slip inside the office."

Okay, Rachael thought. Things were getting out of control here. Two weeks had passed since Mara Lago and that night on the beach. She wasn't sure how Nate found the time to drop what he was doing to fly from Miami to West Palm to accommodate her schedule. The private jet helped. So did his money. Just as both helped to continually remind her that they were worlds apart in every way that counted.

"You're making too much of this. We're just…enjoying each other's company," Rachael assured Sylvie. And that was the sum total of what was happening between them. She'd insisted.

On the long walk on the beach that night, she'd stumbled over her better judgment when she'd agreed to get to know him better, but she'd righted herself again by the time he'd delivered her to her door.

"We have to have finite ground rules," she'd insisted as she fit her key into her lock, aware of his dark eyes watching her.

He'd turned her toward him, cupped her shoulders in his big hands. They'd felt warm and strong and she'd fought an almost irresistible urge to ask him to slide those capable hands down her arms, around her waist and pull her snug against him.

"Ground rules?" he'd asked with a puzzled quirk of his brow.

"I've already told you, Nate," she began with as much steely resolve as she could muster. "I don't do well with relationships. So let's not try to make this into one, okay? I want to make sure it's understood that when it runs its course and one of us is ready to call it quits, the other agrees to walk away. No harm. No foul. No bad goodbyes."

His eyes had darkened in both confusion and challenge. "What makes you so sure it's going to end in goodbye?"

That one had been easy to answer. "Because it always ends in goodbye."

He'd watched her face for a long time, measuring,

clearly wondering, but he hadn't argued and he hadn't asked why she was so sure. He'd only squeezed her shoulders and said, "Let's just take it slow and see where it goes, okay?"

"And what if it doesn't go where you want it to? What if I said I'm still not sure I'm going to sleep with you?"

She'd figured that question would put the skids on things. She'd held her breath in both anticipation and dread of his reply.

"Then I'd say I'll hang around until you make up your mind."

She'd blinked up into his eyes, realizing she had no clue what made this man tick. "I haven't even been nice to you. Why do you want to do this?"

"You're right. You haven't been nice," he added smiling that infuriating, wonderful, patient, penetrating smile. "Just imagine the possibilities when you finally decide I'm not such a bad guy after all."

She'd looked up at him, studied his face wondering, who is this man?

"You'll need to give me a sign, though."

His non sequitur threw her even more than the soft look in his eyes. "A sign?"

"When you make up your mind. To let me make love to you."

He'd surprised her yet again. He was supposed to push here. He was supposed to shove a little and say Hey—no sex, no deal. It had been an unspoken but assumed condition of any relationship she'd ever been in. But then, she reminded herself—this wasn't a relationship.

She couldn't help it. She'd stretched up to her tiptoes, touched her fingers to his strong jaw and kissed him. "Believe me," she'd said, forcing herself to pull away after a little sample of his mouth when what she'd wanted was a long, satisfying feast, "you'll be able to figure it out if and when I do.

"Good night, Nate," she'd whispered and slipped into her town house. "And thanks. For Mara Lago."

He'd shoved his hands into his pockets. "My pleasure."

He was still standing there, watching her with a probing frown when she'd closed the door.

"Houston...do we have a problem?"

Rachael dragged herself away from the memory of that night and tuned in to Sylvie's amused smile.

"No. We do not have a problem."

"So...it's going well then?"

"Don't make more of this than it is," she repeated, recognizing Sylvie's speculative look and knowing she was seeing things that were not meant to be. What was meant to be was that Rachael was destined to go it alone. She'd learned that lesson early on—from her father and her mother and then from her own inability to relate to the men in her life. She couldn't be what they needed her to be.

She had to remind herself of that very thing every time Nate picked her up to take her to dinner, or to a movie, or kayaking or just for a long drive. Don't make more of this than it is became her mantra as she worked constantly to remind herself just to enjoy the moments with this man.

Just because they liked the same music and the same movies and fast food and Mara Lago—fast food and Mara Lago, now there was a study in contrasts—

and just because he made her smile and had honored her wishes and not pressed her about a physical relationship in their non-relationship, it didn't mean anything.

The truth of the matter was—and she was ticked with herself because of it—she sort of wished he would push a little in that area…the one that had to do with a bed and him and her in it. Talk about not knowing what she wanted. He'd been the perfect gentleman. Hadn't done more than drop a chaste kiss on her cheek when he'd walked her to her apartment door each night.

It was what she wanted, right? No pressure. No messy complications.

When her phone rang, she was relieved for the distraction until Sylvie announced the caller.

"Mrs. Buckley," Sylvie said with a sympathetic smile and handed her the receiver.

Rachael suppressed a groan then listened and made notes as the Palm Beach matron made several more changes to her daughter's wedding plans.

She looked like a sea nymph, Nate thought, watching Rachael where she sat on the foredeck, her hands propped behind her for support, her fingers wrapped around the cleats of the little Sunfish he'd rented for the afternoon. Like some mystical creature spun from legends and myth and midnight dreams of a lonely seafarer's obsession with romance.

And he was, in a word, spellbound. Had been— just as he'd been looking at her in a different light— since that night on the beach when she'd agreed to let him start over with her.

*No regrets. No bad goodbyes.*

He'd thought about what she'd said often, wondered often, what had prompted her to say it—and to sound so certain she knew what she was talking about. But today, he was simply thinking about today and the way she looked.

Despite the drying power of the warm Florida sun, she was soaking wet from his last little stunt that he hoped to hell she'd never catch on to. The wind dragged her sodden hair back from her face. The sun and excitement had painted her cheeks a berry-pink. And the look of wonder on her face had had him grinning for the better part of the afternoon.

"This is so wonderful!" she shouted above the whip of the wind and the snap of the sail as they scooted across Lake Worth.

"Yeah, well, you weren't saying that five minutes ago when I landed you in the drink," he reminded her and had the pleasure of seeing her blush then laugh and look out across the lake as if she were seeing the world—or this part of it—for the first time.

She'd been a sport, though, once she'd realized they weren't going straight to Davy Jones's locker. He'd turtled the little sailboat twice since they'd hit the water a couple of hours ago. They'd flipped once by accident—if you could call his preoccupation with the look of her an accident. The second time, he'd done it on purpose.

He'd had so much fun treading water alongside her the first time as they'd clung to the capsized sailboat, his arms circling her to reassure her, their bare legs brushing against each other under water as they flutter-kicked to stay afloat, he'd felt the need of an excuse to do it again.

And then of course, there had been that exquisite opportunity to have a legitimate reason to cup her sweet little tush in his palms after he'd righted the craft and given her a helpful, but lingering push to get her back aboard.

"You're a sick man, McGrory. Copping a feel like a schoolboy," he muttered under his breath, but he was grinning as he adjusted the sail and set an easterly tack.

He felt a little like a schoolboy around her. A little nervous even and it was one sharp kick in the keister to admit it to himself. But he didn't want to blow it with this woman. She was loosening up but she was still a little skittish. Damn. He just kept going back to his gut feeling that someone must have done a number on her.

And she, intentionally or not, was doing a number on him. He'd never been in such a chaste relationship with a woman. Not that he saw sex as the be-all and end-all, but with the chemistry zinging between them, he was champing at the bit to take what they had to the next level. He enjoyed the hell out of being with her. She had an irreverent sense of humor, shared his passion for movies and music and she was quickly becoming enamored with some of his favorite sports. Like snorkeling and kayaking and today—sailing.

"You've lived in Florida *how* long?" he asked, still amazed at the sun-and-fun sports she'd never let the closet adventurer inside her indulge in. "And you've never been sailing until today?"

These were the kind of things that constantly

amazed him about her. Okay. So there was nothing amazing about the fact she'd been born in Ohio and moved with her single mom to Florida when she was just a little kid. What was amazing were the little bits and pieces of herself she parted with in those moments when she let her guard down enough to give them up. What was amazing was how little fun she'd allowed herself in her life—and how much information she still shielded from him.

A private person was Ms. Matthews, he thought, watching her lift a hand to her hair to drag an errant strand away from her mouth. His heart flat-lined, then picked up the beat again with a thudding ker-whump when she kept her arm raised, elbow to the sky, holding back her hair, effectively making her back arch and her sweet breasts thrust against the skyline and press against the cups of her black swimsuit. Her nipples poked against the thin, wet fabric like hard little diamonds.

He wanted to feel them poking against his tongue. He wanted to taste them. And then he wanted to taste the rest of her.

The woman was built like a centerfold. Small, delicate and stacked. Before today, he'd gotten lasting impressions of her drool-worthy body, but there was something about her today. She was relaxed and beautiful and the really amazing part of it all was that she was oblivious to how exotic and enticing she truly was. And about how hard he got just thinking about her coming apart beneath him.

The punch of lust he'd been fighting for the better part of the day—hell, who was he kidding? He'd been fighting it ever since he'd met her—hit him with the wallop of a Patriot missile. A man could only take so many pecks on the cheek at the end of an evening before he started suffering from SRS—sperm-retention syndrome.

And there was only one thing to do about it right now. With the flick of a hand and the tug of a rope, he flipped them into the water again.

"Whoops," he said, as he surfaced and saw her treading water in front of him.

Laughing, she dragged wet hair away from her face with one hand and clung to the side of the overturned boat with the other.

"You are either *really* bad at this or *really* good," she said and surprised him when she reached out and finger-combed his hair back and out of his eyes. "I haven't decided which."

He took advantage of a rocking wave that tossed him closer, until they were practically breast to chest in the water. And then he took heart in the look in her eyes and the lingering touch of her hand, drifting to his shoulder now, to close the small distance between them.

"It does make a body wonder if I really know what I'm doing, doesn't it?" he murmured, transfixed by the spiky wetness of her lashes and the sudden and unmistakable heat in her eyes.

"On second thought," she whispered as he wrapped an arm around her waist and pulled her the rest of the way toward him—until the cool resilience of her thighs brushed against his under the surface and the supple buoyancy of her breasts nestled against his bare chest. "I think maybe you know exactly what you're doing."

He searched her face, then dropped his gaze to her breasts, plumped and pressed against him. He swallowed. Hard. Met her eyes again as the water lapped around them and sunlight glinted like diamonds on the gentle chop. "Yes, ma'am. I believe I do."

And then he kissed her.

The way he'd been wanting to kiss her since that day he'd claimed her mouth on the seawall.

Open-mouthed, seeking tongue, unleashed need.

She was so wet, her lips so cool. But inside, beyond the water-chilled softness of her incredible lips, her mouth was hot. And open. And willing, as her tongue tangled with his and she told him without words that she was as needy and as thrilled by the contact as he was.

With a low growl, he let go of the boat and wrapped both arms around her. Tunneling one hand up and inside the high-cut leg of her suit, he cupped her bare bottom in his palm. When she slid her leg up and along his, hooking it around his hips, he pressed her against the monster erection nestled against her belly and ravished her mouth with a hunger that, if he'd had his wits about him, would have scared the ever-loving hell out of him.

He heard a gurgling, "Yikes," against his mouth just as their heads sank under the surface of the water.

It wasn't until she started pushing away and kicking that it registered he might manage to drown them out here yet if he didn't get his senses about him.

With a firm grip around her waist, he kicked to the surface. They broke water with gasping breaths.

"God. I'm sorry. You okay?" He held her against him, cupping her pale face in his palm.

"Umm…well…I guess that depends."

He tilted his head. "On?"

"On whether you're too waterlogged to swim that far." She notched her chin toward the far distance behind him.

His wet hair slapped against his forehead as he whipped his head around. The Sunfish had drifted a city block away while he'd been leading with his libido.

He scrubbed drops of water out of his eyes, faced her grimly. "I'm some fun date, huh?" he asked, bemoaning his stupidity.

"Yeah," she said softly, and, after a prolonged moment, smiled. "You're some fun date."

With her eyes on his, tentative, searching, she pushed away then started swimming toward the capsized boat.

He trod water for a long time, feeling every heartbeat, watching her long, strong strokes, wondering what that kiss had meant. Wondering what the look in her eyes had meant. Wondering if he knew—really knew—what he was getting into with this woman.

She did things to him. With a dewy look. With an innocent touch. With those shuttered green eyes. She held secrets behind those eyes and harbored a pain he wanted to make go away but suspected he might, one day, contribute to. And that notion made him angry. At himself. At whoever had hurt her.

What do you want from her? he asked himself as he started swimming after her. What do you *really* want?

The word *forever* echoed through his mind, like the

wail of a fog-shrouded lighthouse warning—distant, out of focus, out of bounds.

*Forever.*

Not possible. There was only one woman he'd ever thought of in those terms and she was forever out of his reach.

Later that day, after Nate had dropped her off at her town house, Rachael stood under the shower in her bathroom, washing sea salt and sunscreen and the scent of Nate McGrory from her skin.

Him and his teasing smiles and gentle patience when he'd tried to teach her the basics of sailing. He seemed infinitely patient, a fact that endeared him to her so much more than she wanted. Patience wasn't one of her best virtues, so his fascinated her.

So did his kisses, she thought with a deep breath and shivered under the steaming hot spray. Low in her belly, heat pooled, along with a deep aching need that grappled for control over her better judgment. She could still see him there on the Sunfish—his strong face tipped to the wind, his capable hands working the rudder and the sail. He'd been tanned and lean and muscled in all the right places—especially when he'd hoisted himself up and out of the water and back into the boat. His shoulders were so broad, his hair so black, his lashes long and spiky wet as she'd watched his face. As he'd lowered his head to kiss her.

She remembered every moment of the day they'd spent together on the water. In the water. Under the water. And prayed for the strength to keep herself out from under him.

It would be…wonderful between them. She knew that. His kisses had shown her exactly how wonderful. He was thorough with his mouth. He liked to take his time. Liked to seduce her by white-hot degrees with the playful swirl of his tongue, the subtle—and not so subtle—nudge of his hips, before he showed her what he really had on his mind.

And yet, he never pushed, didn't demand, she realized as she soaped her breasts and shuddered as the brush of her fingers over her nipples made them tighten, and pucker and long for the warm wetness of his mouth there.

The kiss they'd shared had been spontaneous. He hadn't maneuvered her into it this time as he had the first time on the seawall. It had just happened.

She tipped her face to the spray for a final rinse then twisted off the faucets and stepped onto cool white tile. Wiping steam off the vanity mirror with a towel, she studied her face. Despite the color the sun had painted on her cheeks, she looked pale, weak even.

"Weak-kneed," she grumbled as she dried off then grabbed the hair dryer. "And weak-willed," she muttered, shutting off the dryer and bracing her palms on the vanity. She lowered her head in defeat.

She was going to make love with him. The next time he came to see her, she was going to take the chance. And damn the consequences.

A spiral of longing licked through her, starting at her breasts and fanning out to her extremities like a liquid sunburst on a hot August morning.

She shook her head.

She'd never wanted, never needed, never hurt this

much for the touch of one man's hands. One man's mouth.

"Sex," she declared, straightening with a resolute set of her shoulders, "does not have to lead to anything but...more sex," she reasoned, warming to her argument—and to the thought of his mouth on her body.

Her nipples puckered again, tightened, just thinking about it.

She knew the score going in, didn't she? She knew they weren't talking about love. She knew that love wasn't something to count on even if they were.

"Well, don't you?" she snapped at her reflection and, snagging a bottle of lightly scented lotion, slathered it over her sun-warmed and arousal-flushed skin.

"Yes. I do," she assured herself and walked into her bedroom to slip into panties and bra. "I know that."

So what if she liked him. A lot. So what if he listened to her, asked her about herself as though he was interested—really interested—in what she'd done in her life, what she liked, what she thought? He'd lose interest soon enough when he got to know her. Or rather, when he realized he was never going to get to know her.

It had been a long time since she'd wanted to open herself up to a man. A long time since she'd thought she could trust a man that much. But she knew herself. She knew she'd freeze up and freeze him out. It's just the way she was. And she didn't know how to be any different. Not be any different and protect herself in the process.

She'd wanted to believe in love once. She'd wanted

to believe she'd find it. But long before Nate Mc-Grory had come into the picture, she'd accepted that it was never going to happen for her.

And if she had any false and fleeting illusions about it happening with Nate all she had to do was log on for a little reality check. Other than their single status, their close proximity in age, and, well, the fact that he seemed to enjoy her company as much as she enjoyed his, they did not have one single thing in common except chemistry.

He lived in Miami. He flew in private jets, for God's sake. Per the society magazines, he had women flocking around him like flies. And he liked his life that way.

Not wanting to be alone with her thoughts anymore, she grabbed her phone and dialed Kim's number.

"Hi," she said, when Kim answered. "Wanna go to a movie or something?"

"Sure," Kim said. "What do you want to see?"

Something to take her mind off Nate McGrory's slow hands and hot mouth.

"Anything but a chick flick," she said resolutely. The last thing she wanted to see was a movie where the girl got the guy in the end.

# Eight

His momma would be proud of him, Nate thought with a frustrated groan a week after their sailing adventure. He was back in West Palm, approximately twenty steps away from Rachael's bedroom, a few weeks into their nonrelationship, and it was still as pure as the driven snow. Actually, some snow right now might not be a bad idea. Right down the front of his pants. He could use something to cool himself down.

"I'm out of merlot but I've got a nice pinot noir," she called out from the kitchen where he heard cabinet doors open and close and the tinkle of wineglasses as she slid them from the rack.

"Sounds fine."

It was Friday. They were at her town house. He was sitting outside the open sliders at a glass-topped table on her lanai, absently thumbing through a Ludlum novel she'd left on a table beside the chaise, waiting for her to join him. After their afternoon on the sailboat last week, they'd made plans to attend an outdoor festival at City Place Plaza tonight. He'd flown in this morning for a business appointment and had finished up early.

After he'd checked into his hotel, showered and changed into a white knit polo shirt, tan shorts and sandals, he'd killed a little time on Worth Avenue. Then he couldn't stand it a minute longer. He'd taken a chance and dropped by early knowing she'd have just gotten home from work.

She'd been surprised when she'd answered his buzz a few minutes ago. It had shaken her composure a bit, seeing him standing there, unexpected. That was good. Ms. Matthews was entirely too controlled and too in control to suit him and he figured rattling her a bit was good for her. Maybe good for him, too.

He liked the look of her. She hadn't been home long. She'd ditched her blazer and tie but still wore her skirt and white blouse. The top two buttons were undone. That little concession to comfort shouldn't have made his pulse leap—neither should her bare feet—but they had. Couple those two seemingly austere elements with the little bit of white lace peeking from above the southern-most open button and he'd been pretty much buzzed on the thought of flicking open a couple more.

It said a lot about his state of mind—and his unraveling self-control.

"I don't suppose you've got anything to eat?"

It had come to that. He had to do something with

his hands or when she walked out here, he was going to drag her onto his lap, grind her sweet little hip against his erection and let her know just exactly how much he wanted her. A wineglass in one hand, food in the other and his mouth full ought to keep him busy and the footing on her terms, which were getting harder and harder—no pun intended—to keep.

"Did you miss lunch?" she asked from the kitchen.

If only it was that simple. "Just got the munchies." For her.

"Okay—I think I've got—"

He heard her refrigerator door open then close.

"Yes. I've got brie and crackers."

"That'll do it."

It would have to. The past weeks had been some of the most fun, most surprising—most sexually frustrating—of his life. Being with her and not having her was killing him. But, he had to admit, being with her without indulging in a physical relationship had also been enlightening. He'd learned things about her that he might not have if they'd spent the kind of quality time he'd have liked to in her bed.

For instance, he'd learned that little Miss Rachael was a very sentimental person. She teared up at spectacular sunsets, wouldn't visit a pet store because she couldn't bear to see all those poor little kittens and puppies needing homes. And then there was the other side of her—the one well-versed on both domestic and foreign affairs—they'd had some thought-provoking and heated debates. She volunteered what time she could spare at a women's shelter. That one had really gotten to him. It made him wonder about her childhood, and had him worrying about what she might have lived through. Some day he would ask her about it. In the meantime, he'd take what he could get.

She was a voracious reader—everything from biographies to do-it-yourselves to cloak-and-dagger to romance. She was a contradiction, in more ways than one and for some reason, the romance section of her bookshelf gave him hope.

Her eclectic decorating style reinforced his growing conviction that at heart she was a sensualist. She clearly loved bright colors and soft fabrics, airy open space and modern art. Scented candles and sumptuous desserts. Even out here, on the lanai, she'd surrounded herself with hibiscus, bromeliad and any number of brightly flowering plants that scented the late afternoon with exotic fragrances. Sensual, he thought again—right down to her love of salsa music. He was dying by degrees to see her let loose and give him a private showing of that side of her.

She walked out onto the lanai then. Without a word, she slid a plate of cheese and crackers in front of him and set a glass of wine on the table.

The air seemed to crackle between them as she accidentally bumped his shoulder.

"You're sure it's all right that I'm a little early?" he asked, when she pulled quickly away. Had she felt it, too? How could she not have felt it?

"No. No that's fine. I'll…I'll just jump in the shower quick, if you don't mind waiting."

The huskiness in her voice skittered across his senses like a live wire. So did the thought of her slipping out of her skirt and blouse—then standing beneath the hot fingers of the shower spray. Every muscle in his body clenched at the image of her soap-slicked breasts and rivulets of water sluicing between them, past her navel and lower.

He didn't look up. He didn't dare. He wasn't sure he could keep his hands off of her if he did. "Fine. Great. Take your time."

He downed a huge gulp of wine as he heard her bare feet slap softly across the tile on her kitchen floor. Then he stuffed some crackers into his mouth.

Something had to give. Soon. Or he was going to burst a vein.

Rachael turned off the shower and with an unsteady hand, hooked a towel and wrapped it around her, securing it above her breasts. Her heart danced to a hard rock beat—which was a little disconcerting considering she'd slipped a sultry Latin guitar track into the CD player in her adjacent bedroom before hitting the shower. Her legs felt weak as she stood in front of the bathroom vanity mirror and thought about the man waiting for her on her lanai.

Dark eyes, sleek muscles, barely veiled desire.

It was all there when she looked at him. He wanted her.

And, oh, my—mistake or no mistake—did she ever want him.

She might have made up her mind last week that tonight was the night things were going to change between them, but it didn't diminish the impact of the step she was about to take. Or relieve her of her jitters. She'd had the entire week to acclimate herself to the idea and convince herself she could do this. She could enjoy a physical relationship—there was that word again—with this attractive, attentive man and when it ran its course, she could walk away from it without regrets.

She'd had it all planned. When he arrived tonight, she was going to meet him at the door wearing her red sequined Spandex number. He'd have taken one look, known what she had in mind and that would have been the end—or in this case the beginning—of that.

Only he'd shown up early, knocked her off her stride. Now she wasn't entirely sure how to proceed. He wasn't going to make the first move, that was for sure. He was a man of his word, Nathan McGrory. She'd said hands off until she gave him a sign and except for that blistering kiss in Lake Worth last week, he'd played by her rules.

Those stupid rules had only made her crazy with wanting him, achy with need. And suddenly, she was very decisive.

She toweled herself dry then slathered her legs and arms with lotion spun with essence of melon and strawberries and flowers and cream. She didn't bother to dry her hair but brushed it back from her face instead. With the determination of a woman on a mission, she dropped the towel and slipped into her short green silk kimono.

Pushing back all self-doubts, she shrugged off distant warnings that she was going to live to regret this. With one last look in the mirror, she stepped out of the fragrant, steam-clouded bathroom and into the last thing she needed…and the one thing she wanted as much as she'd once wanted someone to love.

* * *

Nate heard the bedroom door open and steeled himself. Rachael's scent floated ahead of her into the living room where he'd been prowling around like a restless cat for the past quarter hour. Whatever mind-altering female concoction she'd drenched herself in made him think of jasmine and fruit, fragrant, juicy fruit, and damn if the thought of licking mango juice from her breasts didn't materialize in vivid color in spite of his Herculean efforts to keep it at bay.

"You're a bigger man than this, McGrory," he muttered under his breath. Yeah, and growing bigger by the minute.

Ignoring his altering body parts, he sucked it up, shoved his hands in his pockets and feigned total absorption in the brush strokes and unique style the artist had rendered on the unframed canvas hanging above the credenza in her dining area. The oil painting was all slashing color and sweeping lines. Vivid. Bold. Sensual. Like Rachael.

He glanced at the bowl of fruit on the island counter that separated the open living area from the kitchen and thought about sex. Noticed the ice tongs in the dish drainer and thought about sex. Hell. He could understand the sensuality in oranges—but in silverware, for Pete's sake? He swung back around toward the living area then froze when the soft sound of her bare feet on the white Italian tile floor behind him stiffened his shoulders.

"Nate?"

He braced, wrapped his mind around the idea that they were about to spend another platonic evening sampling local cuisine at the open-air festival. They'd be surrounded by hundreds of people, cocooned in the safety of numbers in a very public place.

"All set?" he asked and as mentally prepared as he could get, turned to the sound of her voice…and felt the earth—or this little patch of it—cave away like a landslide beneath his feet.

She was not all set. She was *so* not all set. Not by a long shot. She wore a short green robe—and from his initial assessment, nothing else.

The long-sleeved robe was the cool, shimmering green of her eyes. Silk, he guessed. It hit her mid-thigh. It hit him dead center in his libido.

He swallowed, his gaze tracking up that expanse of smooth bare thigh to the wide sash she'd belted loosely at her waist. So loosely the lapels lay open in an enticing *V* that closed low and gaped slightly in the valley of her breasts.

Her breasts. He'd fantasized about her breasts like this. Unbound. Full. Shifting with a subtle and evocative little jiggle with every step she took toward him. Tight little nipples pressed shockingly against the fabric.

He swallowed, and turned as hard as stone.

"I…umm…need a little help," he heard her say through what sounded like an underwater tunnel.

He clenched his hands into fists inside his pockets and dragged his gaze away from her chest to her liquid-green eyes. Eyes he could drown in. A body he could lose himself in.

"Help?" he finally managed but it came out more plea than question.

"With this…if you wouldn't mind." She stopped by the island counter, extended an uncapped bottle of lotion. The scent of it and of her, fogged his already overloaded senses. "I can't reach my back."

"Help." Definitely a plea this time as he closed the distance between them. He latched on to the bottle with numb fingers then watched, in sensitized silence as she presented him her back.

He was still standing there, his brain synapses trying to snap back together when she shrugged the robe off her shoulders until it sagged in gentle folds to expose the creamy length of her bare back. Slim. Elegant. He swore he could count each vertebra. Wanted to. Using his tongue.

Clutching the robe together in front with one hand, she lifted her wet hair off her neck with the other and looked over her shoulder—her bare, silky shoulder—at him.

Waiting.

Expectantly.

"Nate?"

He swallowed a lump of longing as his eyes tracked the sleek lines to the small of her back where her slim hips, barely covered in green silk, flared gently.

She said his name again before he found it in him to croak out a rusty, "Yeah."

"In case I'm not making myself clear…that sign you said you needed? Well…you do understand that this is it, right?"

His heart slammed him a good one, right in the back of his sternum. He smiled then, and visibly relieved, she did the same.

"Yeah." He cleared the corrosion out of his throat and moved up close behind her. "As bricks go, it's a big one.'' As in, she'd just hit him over the head with a whopper.

He closed his eyes, breathed her in, then lowering his head, touched his mouth to her exposed nape. Lingered. ''You make me thick-headed, Rachael. You make me crazy.''

''Yeah…well, I'm feeling a little crazy, too.''

She was uncertain of this, he realized through the fog of sensual heat. And feelings so tender, so unexpectedly protective surged ahead of his desire.

''You're sure about this?'' he whispered against her skin, praying her answer was yes, knowing he was only so strong, fast getting intoxicated by the possibilities her invitation implied.

She sighed, a silky, surrendering sound and leaned into him when he slid a hand around her waist, squeezed gently. Setting the lotion on the counter beside them, he spread the fingers of his other hand wide across her firm abdomen and pulled her back against him.

''Yes, Nate. I'm sure.''

And in this moment, Rachael had never been so sure of anything in her life. She closed her eyes, confident of her decision. Surrendering to the delicious reality of Nate finally holding her in his arms, she glided into the moment like a skydiver in free fall.

''We're going to be so good together,'' he whispered against her skin, tracking a string of slow, biting kisses along the curve where neck met shoulder. She shivered and he buried his face in her damp hair.

''I've wanted this…'' he let his words trail off, and she could feel the effort it took for him to slow things when she'd have been pleased as punch if he'd back her up against the wall and take her hot and hard and fast. "I've wanted this for so long." His voice sounded strained, as thick with arousal as the erection she felt nestled against her bottom.

She made to turn in his arms, but he held her still.

"Oh no," he whispered. "Now that this is finally happening, I plan to take my sweet time with you. We're in no hurry here."

A nervous laugh slipped out. "Speak for yourself."

Her put-upon objection earned a low chuckle that rumbled against her neck as he nuzzled her there and made her shiver again.

"You think that after all this time, I'm not going to make this last? I'm going to make love to you slowly, okay? I'm going to wring out every possible response from your sweet little body and then...you know what I'm going to do then, Rachael?"

His breath was a sultry promise. His question a threat she couldn't wait to experience. She sucked in a harsh breath when he nipped the tendon along the side of her neck beneath her jaw then soothed the tiny sting with the wet slide of his tongue. "I'm...I'm afraid to ask."

His big hands spanned wide over her pelvis, pressing her tighter against him. "Be afraid, Rachael Matthews. Be very, very afraid...because when I'm done...I'm going to start all over again."

Her knees turned to pudding. One hand held her snug against him, holding her upright. The other skated slowly up her body, skimmed past her waist then up between her breasts. Fingers spread wide, he clasped her jaw and tipped her head up and back, forcing her to meet his gaze.

His dark eyes smoldered. His lashes dropped to brush his cheeks as he lowered his head and covered her mouth and seared her with a kiss that was all heat, raging and real.

He opened his mouth wide over hers, demanded she do the same, then ravished her mouth with a marauding tongue that plundered and withdrew then plundered again. He drew her with him into an inferno of desire that transcended thought, outdistanced simple need and sent a shock wave through her blood that burst through her body in spikes of molten pleasure.

With his fingers still bracketing her jaw, he lifted his head. Breathing heavily.

"Yikes," she managed with a shaky breath, then had to clutch the island counter to keep from collapsing like a rag doll when he released her.

"I think," he said, his voice husky as he reached for the lotion and poured some into his palm, "you said something about needing some help."

"I...umm..."

"Yeah," he murmured, the fire in his gaze matching hers. "Me, too. We'll get there. In good time. Lift your hair for me, Rachael."

She knew what he saw in her eyes when she met his over her shoulder—she felt shy suddenly, in over her head with this man who had, with one hungry, incredible kiss, melted every bone in her body—but she raised her left arm and did as he asked while clutching her robe together between her breasts.

Slowly, he spread the cool, scented cream from her nape to the sensitive spot between her shoulder blades, then using both hands, he worked the lotion up and over the round of her shoulders.

"Here?" he asked, spreading his fingers over her back then working them around her neck, where he stroked over her collarbone in outward and downward caresses, barely skimming the upper part of her breasts.

She rolled her head and sighed, aching for his clever hands to sweep lower. To touch her breasts. To pinch her nipples between his fingers then turn her and take her in his mouth. She'd never felt so sensitive or so malleable or sensual in her entire life. He could do anything to her, anything, and right now, her only response would be a helpless plea to do it all over again.

"So soft," he murmured as he worked his hands over her skin. Up again, over her shoulders, down her back then slowly upward. She loved the feel of his hands on her, loved the little quiver of anticipation eddying through her body when he worked his thumbs into the tight little knots on either side of her neck.

"Lift your arms for me, Rachael."

She closed her eyes and without a thought of denying him, raised her arms and looped them over his shoulders, loosely clasping her fingers behind his neck.

She didn't think about the fact that they were standing in broad daylight in her kitchen. She didn't think about the very real issue that for all practical purposes, she was totally exposed to him now and he was totally dressed. Her robe hung open, the belt giving up its tenuous link around her waist. The silk slid over her sensitized skin like cool water, making her shiver as he lowered his mouth to her jaw and covered her bare breasts with his hands.

A groan eased out, part relief, part anticipation, all aching need. Finally, finally he was touching her. His big palms cupped and caressed, gently kneaded, reverently shaped and lifted as he pressed her breasts together and fluttered his thumbs over her erect nipples.

She was on sensual overload, barely aware that he'd coaxed her arms down so she could slip off her robe before running his hands along her arms and repositioning them around his neck again.

"I love the smell of you," he whispered and all she could do was watch as he filled his palms with more lotion. "Love the feel of you," he murmured and pressed the center of each palm over her nipples.

She sucked in a breath at the shock of the cool lotion against her heated areolas. And then he was rubbing his hands all over her. Massaging lotion into her breasts, down across her rib cage, then up again, all the way up the length of her raised arms before returning to her quivering breasts.

"Feels good?"

"I...umm."

She felt his smile against her earlobe when he nipped her lightly. "I'll take that as a yes."

He rocked against her, his heat and hardness to her bare back and bare bottom, his hands constantly roaming, arousing, torturing her into gasping little sobs and plea-choked whimpers.

"Nate..."

"Shh…" His breath fanned her nape. "Just go with it. Just…yeah. Just let yourself fly."

One strong arm banded around her ribs, his large palm cupping her left breast, as his right hand forayed lower. She pressed her head back against his shoulder, licked suddenly dry lips as his fingers brushed her curls with lazy, teasing strokes at first until he had her whimpering with frustration. She covered his hand with hers, pressed it against her.

"Please," she whimpered. "Please, please, please."

# Nine

With her hand riding the back of his, he finally cupped her, gently parted her. He slid a finger over her wet heat…and then he did a little groaning, too, as he finessed her body with such utter attention to her pleasure, she thought she'd pass out from the glut of sensation.

"Nate…s…stop. I'm…I…I can't hold—"

"I don't want you to hold back." His breath fanned hot against her ear as he wedged a long thigh between her legs and opened her more fully to his touch. "You're beautiful like this. Let it come, Rach. Just let it come."

To make sure she did, he deepened his touch, working his fingers in and out of her, massaging the sensitive center of all sensation until she climaxed on a ragged sob. Heart pounding, breath clogged in her throat, she poured into his hand and rode with the exquisite rush that rolled on and on and on.

The force of it stole her breath, the intensity robbed her strength and just kept getting stronger. Just when she thought she couldn't stand it any longer, the high ripped through her and finally tumbled her into the steamy aftermath of the longest, strongest orgasm she'd ever experienced.

He held her in silence, letting her recover, letting her slide into the fuzzy glow of mindless completion.

"W-wow," she finally uttered as her head lolled back against his chest.

He pressed a kiss to her temple, tightened his arm around her waist. "You okay?"

She managed a shaky laugh, felt the sheen of perspiration coating her body cool by slow degrees. "I am beyond okay. And utterly selfish," she added with a shiver as he slowly withdrew his fingers from her ultra-sensitized flesh.

"Utterly beautiful." He turned her in his arms. She rested her hands on his chest as he clasped his hands loosely at the small of her back. "Hi." He bent his head to place the most tender of kisses on her mouth.

Not for the first time, she wondered who this man was that he could just give her the most selfless, most incredible sexual experiences of her life and then stand there as if he didn't have a care in the world when his own body had to be screaming for release.

"You," she said, pulling away, and heedless of her nakedness, took his hand and led him toward her bedroom, "come with me."

"Oh, I plan to, darlin'." The wicked grin in his voice kicked up one side of her mouth. "I have very definite plans to do just that. But I'm going to have to make a supply run first." A pained look crossed his face as he stopped her just inside her bedroom door. With a growl, he wrapped her in his arms for a long, hungry kiss.

When he lifted his head and she dragged herself out of another sensual haze, the import of his words finally hit her. "Supply run?"

"You took me off guard, Rachael." His big hands slid down her back, cupped her bare bottom and lifted, pressing her against his erection. "I didn't come prepared to protect you."

She stood up on tiptoe. Pressed a kiss to his mouth. "Good thing one of us planned ahead then, because I don't want you going anywhere."

Unwrapping herself from his arms, she walked around her bed, opened the bedside table and pulled out a box of condoms.

If he was put off by her forwardness, he hid it behind a grin that blossomed beneath the shirt he made quick work of tugging over his head. His sandals and shorts were next. And then his boxers.

She looked from his smiling face to his proud, jutting sex and managed a smile of her own. "Oh. My. Good thing I told them to supersize them."

And then she squealed when he dove over the bed and laughing, snagged her arm and neatly rolled her beneath him.

"About that taking-my-sweet-time thing?" Rising up on one elbow, he snagged a condom, ripped the packet open with his teeth and with fire in his eyes, sheathed himself. "Not gonna happen this time, okay?"

"More than okay." She knotted her hands in his hair, moaned when he pushed inside her in one deep, delicious thrust and wrapping her ankles around his hips hung on for the ride of her life.

How she managed to talk then was beyond her. He filled her completely as he pumped into her, driving her toward another sharp, shattering climax as she gasped each word in cadence to his fast, powerful strokes. "So. Much. More. Than. Okay."

They took it slow the next time. And the next. And it did Nate's heart a whole world of good to know he'd obliterated the proper Ms. Matthews's control each time. He didn't feel so bad himself.

Moonlight danced in through the windows in her bedroom, gilding the room and the woman lying spread-eagled on her stomach in the middle of rumpled sheets. He glanced absently at the clock on her nightstand. It was close to 3:00 a.m. The last time they'd made love had been less than an hour ago. And he wanted her again—even though he felt wasted on the sight and the feel of her and the sultry scent of melon and flowers and fabulous sex.

Incredible. He'd known it would be good between them. He'd never guessed it would be off-the-charts fantastic.

He watched her sleeping face in the subdued light. And felt humbled suddenly by the gift she'd given him. This had been a huge decision for her. And she'd given him more than her body. More than sex. Great sex, he reminded himself, not wanting to minimize the experience for even a heartbeat.

What humbled him was that she'd given him her

trust. If he'd learned one thing about Rachael Matthews in the past few weeks, it was that trust was not something she gave easily. And because she'd given it to him, it compelled him to want to give her something, too. Something that walked like, talked like and looked suspiciously like promises.

And it was those kinds of thoughts that had him wondering just what the hell was going on here. He wasn't in a position to make any promises. A thought of Tia flitted briefly through his mind—and then Rachael stirred. Made one of those soft, sexy kitten sounds that instantly turned him to stone. And he was done thinking for a while. Except about how he could give them both pleasure.

He rose to his knees behind her, straddling her hips and indulged himself with the feel of his hands on her back. Gently stroking, patiently arousing, he woke her with lingering caresses until she reached up with a limp hand and dragged a skein of tousled red hair away from the beautiful face pressed into her pillow.

"Nate?"

He bent over to press a kiss between her shoulder blades then lick his way down those sexy vertebrae to twin dimples at the small of her back. She wasn't the only sensualist in this bed tonight.

She shifted her hips restlessly, then let him lift her, until she was on her knees in front of him, her pretty little bottom so tempting, he bent down to take a taste of it.

"How can I need you again?" he whispered as he rolled on protection, fitting his heat to hers and guided himself to her silken opening. With a groan that transcended pleasure, he entered her, his fingers clutching her hips to draw her nearer as she clawed for purchase on the sheets and took him deep.

His mind was full of her. His body burned for her as he drove into her, set a rhythm as old as time, as natural and pure as breathing. Slowly, he eased them up and over an edge tempered by tenderness, fired by mutual need until they gave themselves over to the sensation and the wonder and the joy.

Exhausted and spent, he lowered her to her side and wrapped himself around her back. He filled a palm with her breast, buried his face in her hair and tried not to think about the emotions churning around in his chest.

Tried and failed even as he drifted closer to sleep. He cared about this woman. A lot. He respected her. Above all, he desired her. And that, Jack, was the only track this train ran on, he reminded himself. It was not the love train. He'd known that going in. He was in love with someone else and Rachael didn't do relationships.

He fell asleep to the rhythm of her breathing, to the gentle thrum of her heartbeat pulsing against his hand. And tried to ignore the hollow sense of emptiness he didn't want to deal with or explore.

It was as if the dam had broken, Rachael thought the next morning as she stood in the shower and felt the sting of last night's activities on her breasts and between her legs. Years of pent-up sexual energy had flooded through her. She'd done things, said things, begged for things she hadn't known she'd wanted or needed or desired. It had been a very long time for her—and in a couple of instances the first time. He was inventive, her multicultural lover.

She'd never been so uninhibited in a physical relationship. Granted, her experience was pretty limited, but still, some of the things they'd done! Her face flushed red as she stepped out of the shower and carefully dried all the tender spots on her body.

Was she sorry? No. Sore? Oh yeah. And it had been worth every moment. She'd suspended reality last night. She hadn't thought about always and forever, no matter how persistently they'd hammered away at her shields. She'd thought about the moment and the night and the man. And she'd made that be enough.

Determined not to have one of those uncomfortable first morning afters, she wrapped up in her robe and followed her nose to the kitchen.

Looking gorgeous and sleep-rumpled and as appealing as the fresh-brewed coffee he'd made, Nate looked up from the stove and grinned.

"Hey," he said softly, his eyes asking a thousand questions.

She ignored the small corner of her heart that melted at the look in his eyes, ignored the gnawing ache that warned her she might be getting in too deep. Easing gingerly onto a bar stool at the island counter, she accepted the mug of coffee he poured for her with a grateful nod.

"Hey, yourself." She nodded toward the stove. "And you cook, too?"

Looking very domestic and very sexy with a spatula in his hand and wearing nothing but his navy boxers hanging low on his lean hips, he walked to her side, touched a hand to her hair. "Hope you don't mind. I'm starved. Thought you might be, too."

"Let me think. Do I mind waking up to freshly brewed coffee and a manly-man cooking my breakfast? I think that falls in the no-brainer category."

He leaned down and kissed her. A gentle, morning-after-the-best-sex-of-her-life-hello of a kiss. His lips were softly swollen, as were hers; his breath carried the faint scent of her toothpaste and coffee and orange juice.

Heat filled her belly and she arched involuntarily toward the hand that tunneled inside her robe to cup her breast with such sweet reverence that tears stung her eyes.

"You okay?" Concern darkened his eyes as he pulled away.

She got a handle on her emotions, then tried not to flinch as she resettled herself on the bar stool. "Never better. You?"

In answer, he returned to his omelette and shot her a killer smile. Smug. Satisfied. Master-of-his-domain type of smile.

You're not going to break my heart, Nate McGrory, she reminded herself. She knew what she was doing.

"What does your weekend look like?" he asked oh-so-casually as he flipped the omelette then popped some bread in the toaster. "Are you working?"

Most weekends, she did do some sort of work related to Brides Unlimited. Sometimes she went in to the office; often she brought work home. Anticipating the possibility that Nate might end up sleeping over, however, she'd cleared her schedule—at least for today. "Actually, no. I'm not."

He gathered two plates from her cupboard, turned with them in his hands. ''Spend it with me.''

Her heart did a little jump start—just to remind her she was treading some dangerous ground here. Just to advise her that as choices went, agreeing to his request would not be a wise one. So why exactly did you clear your schedule?

''Please,'' he added, setting the plates aside and walking barefoot back to her side. He kissed her again with that firm, gentle mouth that had done things to her in the night that made her blush in the light of morning.

Brushing his lips back and forth across hers, he did some pretty effective, pretty sexy and pretty silly wheedling. ''Pretty please?''

Those two words sent a current of sexual heat sizzling from her breast to her belly. Lord, he was beautiful. All golden skin, rippling muscles and inky black hair that hung over his brow à la an Irish-Latino Rhett Butler rake about to ravage the South—or in this case, the square foot of southern Florida on which she sat.

And he was hers for the weekend, if she wanted him. Talk about a no-brainer.

''Well. Since you asked so nicely.''

He kissed her as a reward, leaving her a little dazed, then dished up their omelettes. Setting the plates and silverware on the island breakfast bar, he sat down across from her.

''What would you like to do?''

She lifted a forkful of egg, onion, green peppers and cheese into her mouth then groaned in appreciation. ''Finish this,'' she finally replied and nibbled on the buttered toast he'd placed on the corner of her plate. "It's delicious."

"I mean, *after* breakfast. What would you like to do?"

When she shifted again, a little twinge reminded her of the rigors of last night's lovemaking. This time she couldn't stall the wince. "I think it's safe to say bicycling and horseback riding are out."

He laughed, then slanted her a sympathetic smile. "How about we start with a long, hot soak in your tub?"

Sympathy had laced with heat by the time she managed to meet his gaze. It was all she could do to keep her voice steady. "As appealing as that sounds, I think the *we* portion of the equation might undermine any soothing effect."

He smiled again. "Poor baby. Then how about I run you a bath and while you soak in it *alone,* I'll make a few calls?"

She could have melted right there on the spot. Told herself a lesser woman would have. No man had ever offered to draw her a bath before. And when, after they'd eaten and he'd tidied up her kitchen—another first—he made good on his offer. He filled the tub with fragrant bubble bath and helped her into it after making sure the water was just right. Then he kissed her senseless and walked out of the room.

She was drifting on a fantasy of him love-slave, her slave-master when he popped his head back in the bathroom, his cell phone at his ear. "How much of your time can you give me," he asked, tipping the receiver away from his mouth.

She blinked. "Until Monday morning?"

"Can you make it Monday noon?"

She blinked again, aware of the bubbles dissipating all around her and mentally reviewed her schedule and her sanity. She had two early appointments on Monday. Sylvie could handle both of them. "Sure," she said before she could second-guess the wisdom of her decision.

He grinned that killer grin and talking to what appeared to be his pilot, left the room.

An hour later, while she was still catching her breath and feeling caught up in some Alice-in-Wonderland fantasy, they were airborne in Nate's Challenger, jetting their way to Key West.

The weekend flew by like a dream. From the flight in Nate's sumptuous private jet, to the indescribably beautiful sunset on Mallory Square where street performers delighted the gathered crowd and luxury liners and frigates with sails furled glided in breathtaking silhouette against an apricot and purple horizon, it was a romantic fantasy come true.

They ate cheeseburgers in paradise at Jimmy Buffett's Margaritaville on Duval Street and ate stone crab with their fingers upstairs at Crabby Dicks'. On Sunday they spent hours at Hemingway House then walked the colorful streets packed with shops before renting a convertible and driving back up Highway 1 across the seven-mile bridge to Matecumbe and Islamorada. It was late afternoon before they returned to Key West again.

They lazed in their swimsuits on the sand-covered jetty of the McGrory's private residence until sunset, drinking rum punch and sharing long, languorous kisses. And at night…at night they made incredible love.

It was perfect. The sun. The surf. The man.

And then, like all good things, it was over.

On the flight back to West Palm Monday morning, while Nate went up front and chatted with the pilot, Rachael thumbed through a magazine and grounded herself in some very important facts. It didn't matter that he'd been gentle and fun and kind and attentive and looked at her sometimes as though she was the only woman in the world. It didn't matter that he made love to her as if the act they shared went far beyond the physical to something that had always eluded her.

What mattered was that their weekend together was all about stolen moments in time and that in time, those moments would be over and he would be gone. What she had to keep in mind was that she was most likely one of a long line of women he'd wined and dined and taken on a ticket to paradise.

*Paradise.*

Everyone—especially Rachael—knew that paradise wasn't real. Paradise was an adventure theme park with wild rides and adrenaline highs. Paradise was an illusion. And Rachael saw through all the smoke and mirrors to reality.

The reality was, Nate would leave or she would push him away. The reality was, when that time came, she was not going to let him take her heart with him.

"So…" Tony said, a speculative grin on his face as he and Nate sat at a corner table at the Surf Club bar on Miami Beach Monday night, "I've narrowed this down to cars, money or women."

Nate lowered a brow and considered his brother. Where Nate took after his mother, Tony was the spitting image of the old man. Fair skin, black hair and built like a linebacker—in fact, he'd played linebacker at Florida State. "What? I can't call my brother for a friendly nightcap without an ulterior motive?"

"Well, yeah, you could, but the fact is, you haven't. Not for a long time now."

Nate stared at his tumbler of Scotch on the rocks while rubbing his thumb along the condensation on the glass. A jazz riff, from the piano in the corner of the members-only bar floated on air lightly scented with pricey Cuban cigars. "Yeah," he finally agreed, meeting his brother's solemn face. "It's been too long."

Tony only nodded, lifted his own Scotch to his lips. "So, what's up, little bro?"

Nate rolled his head on his neck, stared past Tony toward the mirrored wall of liquor bottles behind the ornate bar. "How did you know it was love with Tia?"

Tony was quiet for a moment. He slumped back in his chair and pinned Nate with a look. "Are you asking how did I know when I fell in love with Tia or how did I know when *you* fell in love with her?"

Nate felt his jaw drop.

Tony shook his head, laughed.

"You knew? You've *known*?"

"Knew you thought you were in love with my wife? Oh yeah."

Nate sucked in a deep breath. Let it out. "And you didn't punch my lights out. *Why?*"

Tony, in a motion that neither brother realized exactly mirrored Nate's, rolled a shoulder. "Because you were so earnest in your determination to be honorable and not to let it show. Because Tia would have had my head on a platter if I had. And—"

"Wait. Tia knew, too?" Nate felt as though he'd just had a chair pulled out from under him.

Tony's shrug said, 'fraid so. He leaned forward and finished his thought. "And I didn't say anything because I knew you'd eventually figure out you weren't really in love with her."

Nate stared at his brother long and hard. "So why the hell didn't you let me in on this little pearl of wisdom?"

"Why didn't I let you know you weren't really in love with her? Would it have done any good?" Tony snorted affably. "Hell no. One, you wouldn't have believed me. Two, you'd have gone off half-cocked and made yourself even more scarce than you do now and three, I knew you'd figure it out for yourself one day. I'm thinking, by the look on your face, today's the day or something damn close to it."

*Or something damn close to it,* Nate thought, thrown completely off kilter by the way his mind had wrapped around thoughts of Rachael and would not uncoil. And now his brother was telling him he'd known all along about his feelings for his wife. And that those feelings weren't real.

He drained his Scotch in one long deep swallow then raised the glass, ice clinking, to indicate he wanted a refill. He'd barely set the empty back on the table when another appeared in front of him.

"It's damn confusing," he confessed, nodding his thanks to the waiter before catching his brother's amused expression. "Sure. Go ahead. Laugh. I'm a clown. Big whoop."

Tony just shook his head and grinned. "Oh, how the mighty fall. It's entertaining as hell to see the Don Juan of the debutante set twisted up this way."

"So glad to be of service." Nate scrubbed a hand across his jaw. "I think I'll get drunk."

Tony's scowl held little sympathy. "Might do you some good. Nothing like a hangover to make a man humble. And nothing like a woman to drive a man to drink. So, this would be about the elusive Rachael?"

Nate frowned into his glass. "How can I love Tia all this time…and then just…just…hell. What the hell am I *just?*"

The huge sigh Tony let out said Oh for Pete's sake, this schmuck really needs my help and I'm loving it. "At the risk of sounding way too analytical, let me number it off for you again. One, you didn't really love Tia, you were in love with the *idea* of loving her. Two, it was only a matter of time until some sweet little thing made you realize what you'd been missing. And three, you've never really been in lo—"

"Don't say it," Nate cut his brother off with a dark look. "I'm not ready to go there yet."

"So where are you ready to go?"

Nate stared into space, completely baffled. "I don't know. I can't figure it out. I can't figure *Rachael* out. I like her. A lot. I respect her. She's funny and bright and so damn stubborn she makes my teeth ache."

"I'm thinking she makes something else ache, too."

Nate tipped back his head, stared at the ceiling. *Oh yeah.* She turned him inside out with her uninhibited passion.

"So you've got the hots for a spicy little number. It'll pass."

Nate whipped his head to his brother, ice in his eyes.

The jerk laughed. "Whoa-ho. I'm loving this. So, those were fightin' words, huh? Thought they might be."

"I may just have to clean your clock," Nate said, knowing his grin took all the heat out of his threat. "You baited me."

"Yeah, I did. You're so easy. This woman. She's special to you. You just haven't figured out how to deal with it yet."

"What I haven't figured out is how to deal with *her.* She doesn't want a relationship. Works damn hard at keeping her emotional distance—it's like she's determined to prove to herself that what we've got going is based only on physical attraction."

"And you react to this how?"

"I'm afraid to scare her off so I just go with it. Play along with her cavalier attitude, since that's the way she wants it." Unaware, he tapped his index finger in time to the piano music. "Some sonofabitch hurt her," he said decisively. "And she's not about to open up to anyone—me included—and get hurt again."

"Are you going to hurt her?" Tony asked after a long pause.

God, Nate thought and drained his second Scotch, I hope not. "What I'm going to do is give her a little room."

"You're going to quit seeing her?"

"Hell no. I'm just going to play it her way and not crowd her. And maybe, if we take it slow enough we can both figure it out."

He hoped.

Just as he hoped to hell he figured out where this was going.

# Ten

Gusty clouds played a sassy game of peek-a-boo with the midnight moon. Soft light and fragrant scents drifted in through Rachael's open bedroom window from the lanai and splayed in dancing shadows across wildly tangled sheets.

"You...weren't...kidding."

Rachael could hardly catch her breath. A tropical breeze cooled her heated skin as Nate rolled off her with a satisfied groan.

"Kidding about what?"

"Strong—like bull."

Spread-eagled on his back beside her, he laughed tiredly, sounding pleased and smug and not nearly as exhausted as he ought to be. "I wasn't kidding about the other part, either. The part where I promised I'd make you scream."

Oh, yeah. That part. She'd loved that part. And every little part in between since he'd shown up at ten for a late-Friday-night date. He'd brought takeout Chinese and a hunger for something—in his words—a little more filling. Her.

She stretched and sighed and with lazy interest, watched the blades of the Panama fan spin shades of gray across her pearl-white ceiling. "Now you're just bragging, McGrory."

"And you're just…beautiful."

She turned her head on the pillow and met his gaze. The look in his eyes—so tender and so involved…with her…with the moment—said things he couldn't possibly mean. I missed you. I love you.

She pushed the idiotic thought away.

This was sex. Just sex. *Great sex.* That was the arrangement. That was the expectation.

But he'd been elevating her expectations with his unselfish attention to her every need over the past few weeks. He raised them again five minutes later and made her forget to remember to be cautious when he spread his fingers across her bare abdomen. Hiking himself up on an elbow, he leaned over her, pressed a lingering kiss to the soft curls covering her pubic bone.

She lifted her head, met the heat in his eyes as he looked up the length of her body while his mouth moved over her, sensual, stirring and slow.

Stunned and aroused and amazed, she blinked at him. "Again?"

His lips curved into a smile as he cruised over her skin then lightly nipped her hip point. "Again."

She threw her arms above her head, pushed out an exhausted, delighted laugh. "You *can't* be human."

He crawled up the bed, poised over her on all fours, a sleek, powerful cat on the prowl. Lowering his head to her breast, he rimmed her nipple with the tip of his tongue. "So, now you know my secret."

"Your...oh...um...secret?"

"I come from the planet Lexor," he murmured as he moved his attention to her other breast where he played and licked and drove her to a fever pitch of longing, "a star far, far beyond your galaxy, where I was trained from the cradle in the art of pleasuring green-eyed, redheaded women."

A laugh bubbled out, followed by a gasp...then a groan as he suckled her breast and slipped a finger inside her, softly swirling, expertly arousing. "They got any more back home like you?"

He bit her gently then soothed with a languid caress of his mouth. "You couldn't handle any more like me."

She wasn't even sure if she could handle *him.* At the moment, she didn't want to. She was more than content to have him handle her. And...oh...*oh*...he was doing a fine job of it. His mouth teased and caressed and his fingers, long and lean and so deftly skilled, found her most sensitive places.

She watched through passion-glazed eyes as he moved down her body again, shamelessly dug her heels into the mattress and lifted her hips as he made room for his broad shoulders between her thighs. With his gaze heavy-lidded and hot on her face, he tilted her to his mouth, dipped his head, and nuzzled her damp curls.

Her breath caught as he slowly closed his eyes. He was so beautiful it was almost painful to watch as his dark lashes lay heavy on his cheekbones. The picture of hedonistic indulgence, he found the center of her with his tongue—and drove her in long, torturous degrees over yet another edge she'd never been on before.

"Nate," she whispered. He was all she could think about, all she could feel. All she wanted as he gave her pleasure. Unselfish. Uninhibited. And so perfect it hovered just this side of pain.

He drew out sensations so lush and consuming she lost herself to the wonder of it and to his dark beauty finessing her back up that peak again with delicious and dedicated abandon.

His eyes were dark as his face appeared above hers. She cupped his cheeks in her palms, pulled him down to her mouth where she tasted him and herself and everything that was right in the night.

And when he pressed himself deep inside her, in this suspended moment in time, everything—*everything*—was also right in her world.

It wasn't a place Rachael trusted to last. And as she drifted off to sleep that night, she had to remind herself that anything that seemed to be too good to be real, probably was.

"Mrs. Buckley," Rachael said into her headset Monday morning, trying not to panic as Gweneth demanded yet more changes—and these were getting down to the last minute—to her daughter's wedding. It was slated for Saturday, only six days away. "We really must have things firmed up by tomorrow.

"Yes. That's *tomorrow*, tomorrow, but there's no need to panic. Truly. Everything's under control. I would like to suggest something, though, if I may. Why don't you give me a time that's convenient for you to come by my office this afternoon. I'll clear an hour or so and we can review everything in detail. I think you'll feel much more comfortable about your decisions when you see it all laid out with the changes you've made since we began planning." All five hundred changes, she added in a soundless grumble as she propped her elbow on her desk and pressed her fingertips to her temple.

"Yes, two-thirty will be perfect." She made a quick note to have Sylvie reschedule the Lundstrums for Wednesday afternoon and to do something about the thoughts of Nate that kept creeping into her mind. Random thoughts. Nate naked. Nate laughing. Nate feeding her mangos in bed then lapping the juice off her bare breasts, sucking it out of her navel, licking it from her thighs.

"We'll do a complete walk-through," she said, dragging herself back to the moment. "You're going to be surprised how neatly everything dovetails."

The moment the word *dove* was out, she regretted it. She slumped back in her chair, cursed herself silently and listened as Gweneth Buckley requested just one more teensy-weensy change.

"Two hundred doves as opposed to two is an option, certainly," she hedged through gritted teeth. "No doubt, they'd make a spectacular statement, and while traditionally the release of two doves is a metaphor representing the bridal couple's union, it's not a hard-and-fast rule. I wonder, though," she added, praying she could tactfully steer Mrs. Buckley away from certain disaster, "considering we're also releasing butterflies, while it certainly wouldn't be excessive," try *over the top,* she mouthed silently, "it might subtract from the drama of their flight.

"One other thing you might want to think about," she pressed on, praying she was getting through, "is the issue of…how do I put this delicately? Well, to be frank, two hundred birds have the potential to soil a number of designer gowns."

She blinked, then blinked again when Mrs. Buckley crisply advised her she'd simply have to ensure that that didn't become a problem. What? Like there were plugs for these types of things and she, personally, had to install them in two hundred birds?

The customer is always right. The customer is always right. She repeated the mantra for the next ten minutes until she was finally able to get off the phone. She'd pray for a miracle. Like that Gweneth Buckley would get a clue and have a change of heart about the squadron of doves.

She was massaging her temples, working on a dinger of a headache when Sylvie walked into her office, closed the door behind her and looked at her expectantly.

"What?" Rachael asked.

"I've been good, Rachael. I really have. I haven't asked questions. I haven't pried. But I'm popping a seam here, wondering how things are going with God's gift. Are you ever going to give up the details on Nate McGrory, or am I going to have to resort to groveling?"

"You're coming pretty close to it now," Rachael said with a slight arch of her brow.

"Details, Rachael. Please. I need details. Give 'em up before I slip into an info underload stupor."

The devil was in the details. Rachael knew that. And if she let herself think about them, she'd get that achy, empty feeling in her chest and she wouldn't be able to deal with everything on her slate today.

"There's not that much to tell," she lied. Not much but a great guy, great times, great sex worthy of the Book of World Records.

"Didn't your mother ever tell you your nose would grow if you told too many lies?"

If she lost sight of the fact that there was no future with Nate, the mention of her mother brought it back into focus again. She'd never called her mom back. Somehow a month had slipped by and she hadn't found the time to call and reschedule their canceled dinner.

All in all, she was pretty pathetic—she couldn't even extend her trust to her own mother. To her own family. She couldn't trust them to want to be a part of her life. Nate wasn't family. He was just a man. Just a man she could spend time with without falling in love. On that point, she remained rigid. He was just a man whose smile and gentleness and sense of humor she could love without loving him. She could love the way he touched her, love the way he moved inside her. What she couldn't love, wouldn't let herself love, was him. Just as he could never love her if he really got to know her for the coward she really was.

"You're making too much of it, Sylvie," she insisted, looking her assistant straight in the eye. "It'll run its course and that will be the end of it."

And her heart ached, just a little bit, at the thought of that day looming.

She mentally put on the skids. She wasn't going there. Had already worked it out in her head. And she had everything under control. When their fling was over, she would be ready for it.

She didn't need Nate McGrory. She didn't need anybody. She had her job. She'd made it enough before him. She'd make it enough after.


"So, how did the big Buckley event go last night?" Nate asked as he leaned back from Rachael's table the Sunday evening immediately following the Buckley wedding. He lifted his wine to his lips.

"Hitchless," she said with a relieved look on her face. Laughingly, she'd told him about the doves and the potential for disaster. "At least it appeared to go that way. I stayed until after the band played the first few numbers and then left my staff in charge. What a relief to have that one behind me."

"You love the pressure."

"Yeah," she said with a considering smile. "I do. And while I'm not changing history or shaping the global economy, I'm good at what I do. Can't think of anything I'd rather do, in fact—or what I'd do if it wasn't an option for me."

She worked too hard, Nate thought watching her. He'd figured that out over the past several weeks. But she thrived on it, just as he thrived on his packed schedule. He'd never begrudged it until lately. Lately, he'd wanted more time for Rachael. This was the first chance they'd had to get together in a week. He'd been quietly pleased when instead of going out tonight she'd prepared a delicious vegetable couscous and grilled mahimahi. She'd served it, along with a romaine salad, on her lanai.

Relaxed in a gauzy pale-yellow sundress with her bare feet tucked up under her bottom, she looked young and fragile and so much more vulnerable than she'd ever admit to being.

After spending two incredible weekends with her—and before that, as much time as they'd been able to eke out of those busy schedules—Nate knew now just how vulnerable she really was. Not because she showed that side of herself but because she took such pains not to. And because she went to great efforts to avoid letting him too close. She knew damn well everything about his family and he still knew very little about hers.

It didn't take a nuclear biologist to figure out she was intentionally shutting him out of that equation to make sure he couldn't get too close. And that was the rub. He wanted close. After his heart-to-heart with Tony and some serious think time, he'd realized Tony was right. He'd never really loved Tia. He'd loved the idea of being in love with her. The idea of one woman to commit to. Of a home and family to come home to. He hated like hell to admit that big brother had been right, but he was. Nate had never been in love.

Until now.

He watched the woman he loved with quiet eyes as she tipped her wineglass to her lips. He was in love with Rachael Matthews. Over the moon, take the big walk, tell it to the world, in love.

He was pretty sure she was falling or already in love with him, too. Just as he knew she was fighting it with the tenacity of an army Ranger defending his country. Because of her resistance, he knew he had to take this slow and easy or he'd scare her away before she had time to figure out he wasn't going anywhere.

"What?" she asked, and he realized he'd been staring. The quiet, cornered look on her face reinforced just how skittish she was. She'd sensed that his thoughts had turned serious, and she didn't want any part of it.

He let out a deep breath. Smiled. "I was just thinking…" *What would you do if I told you I loved you?*

*Run like a rabbit, that's what she'd do.*

"About?" She tipped her head, suddenly looking a little edgy.

"About…" He almost said it then chickened out. "Dessert."

The slight relaxation of her shoulders showed her relief. "Opps. Sorry. Didn't make any."

So, they wouldn't talk. At least not tonight. There was time. And he had something else in mind for now.

Her gaze tracked him warily as he rose and lifted her out of her chair in one smooth motion. "You *are* dessert, *mi corazón*," he whispered against her mouth. Then, carrying her inside, he walked straight toward the bedroom. "And I think I'm going to need at least two helpings."

"Oh," she said, looping her arms around his neck. "Goodie."

\* \* \*

*Mi corazón.*

Rachael woke up from a dead sleep in the middle of the night. Her heart pounded like a sledgehammer. Her hands trembled. And Nate's words whispered around in her head like a taunt.

*Mi corazón.* My heart.

Sucking in a serrated breath, she sat straight up in bed, dragged her hair away from her face then pressed her palms to her heated cheeks. Felt them cool as the blood drained away.

She'd never had an anxiety attack. That didn't mean she didn't recognize one when she was in middle of it. Her heart fluttered like hummingbird wings. Her hands trembled. She couldn't draw a deep breath. And she was wide, wide awake. And scared.

*Mi corazón.*

His casually spoken words should have drifted away like smoke. They'd meant nothing. It had just been an expression. Yet, hours after he'd spoken them, hours diluted by sleep, they echoed in her head with the same tenacity that had roused her like a fire alarm.

She fought for another breath, willed herself to settle down. This was stupid. It wasn't that he hadn't spoken to her in Spanish before. In the heat of passion, in the middle of a sultry night, his mind as muzzy as hers in the blinding spiral of shared heat and tangled limbs. But that…that had been passion. That had been letting go.

He'd never said such words in the light of day. And just because he had, it hadn't meant anything. She couldn't take them to heart. She was not his heart. She knew that.

*Mi corazón.*

Tears welled. She blinked them back. No, she was not his heart—but somewhere between gentle smiles and sultry kisses, she'd let down her guard so much that she wanted to be.

Her shoulders sagged with the admission. Oh God, oh God, oh God. She was not his heart. But he was hers. She'd let him become hers. The anxiety that had awakened her transgressed to a heartache so powerful it made her chest tight.

Through a glaze of tears, she looked down at him, sound asleep, his dark head on her pillow. He was so beautiful. And she'd let herself fall in love with him.

Her knees were wobbly when she eased quietly out of bed, shut herself in the bathroom and leaned back against the door.

She was in love with Nate McGrory.

For a long time, she stood there in the dark, aware of her pulse pounding in her ears and the breath catching roughly in her throat. She smelled the clean scent of her melon shampoo and the sharp edge of her panic.

Caught up on that unsteady edge, her defenses collapsed. Pressing a fist to her mouth, she willed back tears and latched on to anger instead.

"Damn you," she cursed herself on a tortured whisper. "Damn you, damn you for being so stupid."

How had she let this happen? And what was it going to take to make her quit wanting the things she could never have? A man who could accept what she had to give him. A man who loved her in spite of her inability to open up to him. A man who needed her. A home that felt full instead of empty. A heart that didn't live in fear of being bruised.

She slid down the door to the floor, wrapped her arms around her updrawn legs and dropped her forehead to her knees. For long, lonely moments, she sat there, dry-eyed, the tile cold against her bottom, the door hard against her back, until numbness finally set in. Her armor. Her insulation. She'd fallen into that unfeeling state to protect her for as long as she'd had memories.

Yes, she knew she wasn't a child anymore, shying from the pain her father had inflicted with both his fists and his denial of the love a child was entitled to receive. She knew she wasn't that lost little girl wondering why her mother had turned her back on her, too.

She was a woman. She was stronger now. But she still felt that overwhelming, knee-jerk need to protect herself. And she knew what she had to do.

It was going to be hard to watch him go.

She sat in a chair by the bed the rest of the night, watching him sleep, waiting for daylight, feeling as though a ten-story building had crashed on top of her. Knowing she had to end it now because she wouldn't have it in her to recover if she let it go on any further.

The coffee was brewing when, fresh from a shower and dressed to attend a meeting at the Breakers at 9:00 a.m., Nate walked into the kitchen.

He smiled when he saw Rachael standing with her back to him at the kitchen sink. A punch of tenderness hit him as hard as the fist of lust. Ms. Prim in her royal blue skirt and blazer. He didn't have to wonder what she wore beneath that sedate business suit any longer. He knew. Just as he knew—intimately—all of her soft, tender places, and that if he went to her now and said the right thing, touched her just so, he might be able to convince her he had time to mess her up again before they headed to their respective meetings.

"Good morning," he said, walking up behind her.

She jumped and pressed a hand to her heart.

"Sorry. Didn't mean to startle you. Hey. Hey," he repeated softly when he realized how tense she was. He cupped her shoulders in his hands and turned her to face him. "You okay?"

Her eyes were sober when she glanced at him, then quickly looked away. Her hands were cold as ice when he took them in his. She pulled them away and fussed with filling her coffee mug.

And while he told himself he was overreacting, suddenly he had a really bad feeling about the closed-off look in her eyes, about the way she refused to look at him.

Determined not to leap to conclusions, he crossed his arms over his chest and leaned a hip against the counter. "What's going on, Rachael?"

Her hands were shaking—although she was doing her damnedest to hide it—when she wrapped her fingers around the pastel-yellow mug he'd come to know was her favorite.

"We need to talk," she said and avoiding his gaze, lifted the coffee to her mouth.

"Okay," he said slowly, surprised at how calm he

sounded considering everything about her behavior was setting off warning bells. "Let's talk."

"I think…" she began, still not looking at him as she abandoned her coffee to hug her arms tightly around her midriff, "I think we need to consider cooling things off between us a little."

He stared at her—at the top of her head actually, because she wouldn't, absolutely wouldn't, look at him. "Cooling things off," he repeated, hearing the steel in his voice but not able to curb it as tension knotted in his gut.

Something in his voice must have warned her that if she didn't face him head-on with this, he was going to make her look at him. And that would involve touching and Rachael clearly did not want to be touched by him right now.

She lifted her head, met his eyes. He saw barely veiled panic and stoic determination.

She tried for a tight smile. Failed. "This has been happening a little fast for me so I'm thinking maybe…maybe we should just not see each other…for a while."

He clenched his jaw to keep an expletive from bursting out and fought to hold on to his patience. She's just experiencing a case of cold feet, McGrory. Nothing to panic about. "It's been pretty fast, yeah," he agreed softly. "And pretty good. Damn good," he stated for emphasis. "I'm not sure I see the problem here."

"The problem is, it's been…a little too intense for me. I'm feeling…crowded." She met his cold silence by looking away, her shoulders rigid. "We agreed,

Nate. We agreed going into this that when the time came to end it—"

"Whoa, wait. End it?" He wasn't calm anymore. Every muscle in his body vibrated with the effort of keeping his temper in check. Every muscle in hers was wrapped as tight as the leash he had around his anger. It took everything—everything—he had to settle himself down. "Rachael…why don't you tell me what this is really about."

"It's about what we agreed to," she said, her eyes just shy of pleading. "We both agreed that when one of us was ready to walk away the other would let them go."

"You agreed. I didn't. And I'm not ready to walk away. Damn it, neither are you.

"No," he cut her off abruptly when she opened her mouth to remind him about her terms. "I don't think this has anything to do with what's going on between us. I don't even think it's about our so-called agreement. I think it's about what you're afraid of."

She closed her eyes, her fingers tightened on the arms she'd wrapped around herself. "Please don't let this get ugly."

"Ugly?" He lifted a hand, laughed grimly. "I'm not making it ugly. You are. This is stupid. Rachael, come on. Don't let a case of cold feet keep us—"

"I don't have cold feet. And there is no us. Look. I have an agenda. I have my career and that doesn't allow for relationship-building. I'm sorry. But that's the way it is. We had a fun few weeks, right? It was great. And now it's over."

"Over. Just like that? Just because you're too

scared to see where it's going?'' he demanded, trying to figure out a way to break through to her.

"Because it's over," she insisted, her voice rising, her cheeks flaming pink beyond the pale. "I know this is a news flash for you, but you don't make all the rules. You don't call all the shots. You're the one who started this. And I'm sorry if it upsets you, but I'm the one finishing it."

Anger and, damn it, panic made his voice harsh. "And what if I said, I'm not going anywhere?"

"I'd remind you that we made a bargain."

"Screw the bargain." Nothing had worked so far. Maybe this would. He went for broke. "Rachael...I love you."

She flinched as if he'd hit her. She stared at him for several long, aching seconds before tearing her gaze away. "I think you'd better leave."

Silence shredded the air.

"That's it?" Dumbfounded, he followed her to her front door then watched, disbelieving when she opened it, a blatant invitation for him to go. "I tell you I love you and you open the damn door?"

"Goodbye, Nate."

He scrubbed a hand over his face, settled himself when what he wanted was to shove his fist through the nearest wall. "Rachael. What the hell happened between midnight and now that made you so afraid of me?"

"I am not afraid."

"The hell you aren't. You're scared to death to accept what a good thing we've got going. So scared you aren't thinking straight." He swore softly when she just stood there, resolute in the face of anything he had to say. "You're a lot of things, Rachael, but I never figured you for a coward. And I'm tired of talking to the top of your head, damn it! Look at me. Look at me and tell me you don't want me in your life."

Slowly, she raised her head. Her green eyes looked as fragile as blown glass when they met his. "You need to leave now."

Hopeless. It was hopeless to talk with her when she was in this mindset. She'd closed off completely. He let out a deep breath.

"Fine." He wasn't going to win this round. Not today. "I'm gone. But I want you to think about something. And I want you to admit the truth. This isn't about us. There is nothing wrong with *us*. This isn't even about me. It's about *you*. Someone hurt you. Hurt you bad and you're feeling scared and vulnerable.

"We're all vulnerable, Rachael," he added, feeling such a complex mixture of love and hurt and anger he didn't dare touch her. "You think you've got the corner on that particular emotion? Think again. We are all vulnerable," he repeated, never realizing until this moment exactly how vulnerable he was when it came to her. "Some of us just carry it differently than others."

Her hand clutched the doorknob in a white-knuckle grip as he walked through the threshold then stopped, one hand on the doorframe. He turned back to her. "Who hurt you? Can you at least tell me that?"

"Please…go."

"I can't fight this. I can't fight something that happened before I met you if you're not willing to fight it with me. I can't fix what's wrong in your life if you won't give me the chance to make it right.''

She looked past him to someplace…someplace where he couldn't reach her.

''You know how to get hold of me,'' he said, and after a long, searching look, walked out the door.

# Eleven

"**Y**ou okay?" Sylvie asked gently when Rachael walked into her office at nine that same morning.

So much for hiding her feelings. Sylvie saw right through her. But then, Rachael didn't have the strength to manufacture even a fake smile. Neither did she have the power to handle Sylvie's mothering. "I need to get right on the Buckley invoices, okay? Can you pull the file for me?"

"Honey." Sylvie followed her into her office. "What's wrong?"

Rachael shook her head, felt the tears gather and stubbornly blinked them back. "I'm fine. I just need to work, okay?"

"Okay," Sylvie said carefully. "Just…just let me know…if you need to talk or anything, I'm here."

Rachael swallowed, nodded and tried to show Sylvie with a quick look that she was sorry for being so abrupt, but that she needed some space right now.

She felt as if she'd been gutted. Ripped from one end to the other with a dull, rusty knife. And it was her own damn fault. And Nate's. For making her love him.

*I love you.*

Why had he said that? She stared blankly at the open folder Sylvie laid on her desk. Why did he have to plant the seed, make her wish, make her yearn for something he couldn't possibly mean? People said those words all the time. No one ever meant them. She thought of her mother, of her father who was supposed to love her and had never done anything but hurt her. Yeah. People said "I love you" all the time. It didn't mean anything. Not when they said it to her.

But God, it hurt. She couldn't imagine anything hurting any worse than this.

Steeling herself to believe she'd severed the artery before the cut got too close to her heart, she dug into the file, determined to lose herself in her work.

"Rachael."

She looked up to see Sylvie standing in open doorway.

"Mr. Iverson wants to see you in his office ASAP."

Iverson, as the head of hotel events, was her direct supervisor. "Did I forget a meeting or something?"

"Not that I'm aware of. He probably wants to congratulate you on the Buckley wedding. It was a huge coup for the hotel—could mean lots of future referrals."

"Not to mention the potential for charity functions

and conventions if Gweneth spreads the word to her old-guard friends,'' Rachael added as she rose and headed for the door, back in control. This is what she understood. This is what would always be there for her. Her work. ''I don't have any appointments until this afternoon so take messages and I'll be back when I get back.''

She felt grounded again suddenly. Her work was the one thing she could hang on to. She'd given it one hundred and fifty percent for as long as she could remember. And in the long run, it was the one and only thing she could count on. It was what was going to get her through losing Nate.

''I'm sorry…did you say suspended?'' Rachael stared across Iverson's lacquered desk in disbelief.

The man had the good grace to squirm. ''It's only temporary. Just until we can get to the bottom of this.''

''The bottom of what? I do not understand. Not any of it.''

William Iverson was in his late fifties, slightly balding and in excellent physical shape. He paled beneath his Florida tan and shook his head. ''It's a bitch,'' he agreed in an uncharacteristic lapse of professionalism. ''And I promise we'll get you reinstated…or possibly reassigned to a different position if it comes to that…in a matter of weeks. A month at most.''

''I don't want a reassignment, nor should a reinstatement be an issue. I haven't done anything wrong.'' She rose, paced to the window, her arms tight around her midriff, then spun and faced him again as anger started to outdistance the shock.

"Okay. Let me see if I've got this straight. The Buckley wedding—which I'd thought had gone off without a hitch—had a problem after all. The doves—the number of which Gweneth insisted on using against my advice—did exactly what doves are wont to do and dropped a little unexpected gift on one of Gweneth's fellow Angels of Charity matrons who were in attendance."

"In her hair," Iverson qualified morosely. "And not just a fellow angel, the head angel."

Rachael went on as if she hadn't heard him. "And Gweneth laid the blame for this little faux pas directly on me. And *this* is reason for suspension? Why?"

"Because Gweneth Buckley cannot afford to have egg on her face with her fellow society matrons. And to save face with them—it's worse than death to become a fallen angel—Gweneth has decided to make you the scapegoat. She called not only our manager but several stockholders and demanded that you be let go."

"This is too ridiculous even to consider, let alone act on."

"Rachael—you do understand, don't you, that these women run the Palm Beach economy?"

"Oh, I understand perfectly. And no one has played the society game better than I have to land the Buckley account and give the woman exactly what she wanted. I gave her the perfect wedding—with the exception of her insistence on those damn doves—and what I now understand is that I'm getting drop-kicked out of sight to save her face. I repeat—this is too ridiculous for words."

"I agree, but I'm still under orders to initiate the suspension."

She shot past stunned and raced straight into outrage. "You do realize you're talking lawsuit here?"

"Now, Rachael. It doesn't have to come to that. We can work something out for you."

"Oh, you bet you can. I'll give you a week and then you'll hear from my lawyer."

"Don't do anything rash. Just think for a minute. See it from the hotel's perspective. Do you happen to know how many dollars in revenue Pettibone Pharmaceuticals generates for the Royal Palms annually? Between their seminars and conventions, it amounts to millions. It's possibly as high as fifty percent of the events' take. Do you happen to know Mrs. Buckley's maiden name?"

"Wild guess?" she said sarcastically. "I'm going for Pettibone."

"Exactly. We can't afford to lose their account—and our stockholders know it. Try to understand. I'd give anything if we could make this go away."

"Anything but giving me my job back," she stated flatly.

"Hang in there with us."

"Right. Just like you've hung in there with me."

"So…promotion *and* pay raise?" Sylvie asked anxiously when Rachael returned to her office fifteen minutes later.

She passed Sylvie by, sank down behind her desk and lowered her head to her hands. She felt ill. Physically, mortally wounded.

"Rachael?"

Slowly, she raised her head and with a shaking hand reached into her desk drawer for her purse. "I've been suspended," she said hearing the hollow ring to her voice. "Indefinitely."

"Say what?"

In clipped, precise words, Rachael told her.

"Oh, God, Rachael. This…this is so unfair. Are you saying they rolled over on this—just like that?"

Rachael rubbed her temple with her thumb. "Like a pack of dogs begging for bones."

She rose and shoved her desk drawer shut. She looked around the office, then walked over to the bookshelf. Tucking the picture of her family under her arm, she headed toward the door.

"Rachael?"

She stopped, turned and let Sylvie enfold her into a hug. "Don't let them get away with this."

"I don't intend to. But I've got to get out of here before I do something stupid." Like let them see her cry. It made her angry all over again that a company she'd given her all to could turn their back on her like this.

Beyond devastated, Rachael drove home in a fog. She shut herself inside her town house. The adrenaline rush of shock lasted about fifteen more minutes. Once she was alone, she didn't have to pretend anymore. She didn't have to show the world her strong side.

She cried. She raged. She threw things and cried some more. She sat alone with the shades pulled and her door locked for days. And sank into the deepest, darkest despair of her life.

She missed Nate. Wanted his arms around her. Wanted him to hold her and make the pain go away.

But Nate wasn't the answer. Nate was gone. And he wouldn't be coming back. Just like her job was gone. Everything that she'd worked for. Everything that was important. Gone.

When the phone rang, she ignored it. When Sylvie came to her door, she refused to let her in.

She couldn't. She just couldn't deal with it.

She didn't eat. She didn't sleep. She couldn't stop thinking that the one thing she'd thought she could count on—the job she'd invested her life in—wasn't even safe for her, no matter that she was blameless in this ridiculous turn of events. She'd run Brides Unlimited better than anyone could have.

And what had it gotten her? Beaten and demoralized and completely alone. As she'd always been alone.

It was on the fourth day, when she'd hit rock-bottom, that she finally found the backbone Gweneth Buckley had stolen from her along with her job. She looked at the pathetic lump of humanity staring back at her in her bathroom mirror and made a decision. Grief wasn't going to drive her actions any longer.

She'd needed this time, yes. To mourn. To wallow around in self-pity. But that time was over. She needed to get on with her life—and she needed retribution.

Righteous anger was calling the shots when she picked up the phone and dialed the one person she wanted to believe in above all others.

Nate slumped back in his chair, his suit jacket tossed aside, the sleeves of his white shirt rolled to his elbows, his tie loose. At his left was his chief litigator, Bryan Morgan, at his right, his executive secretary, Clarice Fox. Facing him at the far end of the conference table were the Borlin brothers, his newest clients, who were counting on him to make right the wrong done to them by a patent infringement.

When the intercom light on the phone at his elbow lit up, every muscle in his body tensed. He'd left word with the switchboard that there was only one person whose call was important enough to interrupt him with.

"Excuse me," he said to the group at large. His hand hovered over the receiver for a long second before he snatched it up. "Yes."

"Rachael Matthews on line one, sir."

He let out a breath he'd probably been holding since she'd shown him her door four days ago. "Transfer the call to my office, please. I'll take it there.

"I'm sorry," he said, standing, "I have to take this call. You're in good hands with Bryan," he assured the Borlins and, without another word of explanation, walked out of the meeting.

"Rachael," he said as he dropped into the chair behind his desk. "Hi."

Silence. He could almost see her gripping the phone with white knuckles. And yet he waited. This was her call. This was her move and he needed to let her make it.

"I'm...I'm sorry to bother you at work."

"It's not a bother," he assured her, concerned about the tension in her voice.

"I hope I didn't interrupt anything too important."

Only the potential for a cool half mill in billable hours and a certain court victory. "It's not a problem. How are you?" he asked, missing her so damn much he didn't care if she knew it.

"Honestly? Not so good."

No, she wasn't good. He heard it in her voice along with the tension, and he waited the length of a long breath before she spoke again.

"Nate...I need a lawyer."

Her statement took a moment to assimilate. It wasn't what he'd wanted or expected to hear. Not, I need you, not, please come back to me, but, I need a lawyer. "A lawyer?"

"Other than you, I don't know any. Have never had a need for one. I was hoping you could suggest someone in West Palm I could count on."

He stared beyond the office window to the view of Miami Beach in the distance and tamped down his disappointment. Okay. So she wasn't calling to profess her undying love. But she had called. He'd take what he could get and worry about the rest later. He'd been dying here. By long, slow hours. He missed her. He needed her. He wanted her on any terms, and if he hadn't heard from her by the end of the week he'd planned a trip to West Palm to confront her.

"Tell me what happened."

She did. Concisely, with little emotion in her voice. He listened, taking notes, shaking his head over the inequity, aching for the pain this had caused her and that she tried so valiantly to conceal. He knew what her job meant to her. He knew that they'd taken more than a position and a paycheck away from her. They'd taken her pride. And he was just the man to get it all back.

"I'll fix it," he said simply.

"No. Oh, no, I didn't mean for you to—"

"I'll fix it," he repeated firmly. "I want to do this for you, Rachael. You can trust me to make this right for you."

"Nate—"

But he'd already hung up the phone.

"So that's where that dress went," Rachael muttered to herself as she dug into her guest-bedroom closet. She'd been cleaning for three days straight—three days since she'd called Nate. Four years since she'd seen this particular dress.

It was gray. Tasteful. Understated. *Dull.* She dragged it off the hanger and tossed it toward the bed and the pile of clothes destined for charity. She'd found too many dull drab things in her closets. Had never realized how few bright, flirty, fun things she owned. And she didn't need gray dresses anymore.

She didn't need a lot of things, she told herself staunchly. Dressed in grubby cutoff jean shorts and a baggy tank top, she ambled out into the kitchen to pour another cup of coffee, but then thought twice when she realized it was getting dark. Mostly, what she didn't need was the victim mentality she'd been unconsciously grooming for as long as she could remember. That was all about to change, too. Several days of wallowing around in self-pity then pulling herself out of the muck had been grueling and painful—but they'd also been the best thing that had ever happened to her. It had forced her to deal with her feelings—feelings she'd been sweeping under the rug or ignoring for too many years now.

And it felt good. It felt—great. Freeing. Like the ultimate makeover of her spirit.

Her decor was also due for a makeover, she decided, after taking a quick shower. She dried her hair then slathered on lotion…remembering the night Nate had taken care of that job for her. An arc of pure longing eddied through her body and cut straight to the heart as she slipped into her robe, determined to think ahead from now on, not back.

Tomorrow she would paint. Something bright and fun and very Florida. She was tired of white walls and of sneaking her penchant for color into her life with carefully chosen accessories. Yeah—some of her art was bold. But not enough of her life was. Not nearly enough. Especially now that Nate was no longer in it.

And there was the rub. She'd been careful all of her life. Careful and cowardly. Where had it gotten her? She was alone. She was unemployed. Basically, she was pretty damn pathetic.

Since she'd forced Nate out of her life and she'd lost her job, she'd learned some things about herself—and most of it wasn't pretty. She'd learned even more when she'd faced her oldest demon and called her mother, insisting on a heart-to-heart chat.

That had been three days ago, right after she'd called Nate requesting the name of a good lawyer. Well, she'd gotten one, she thought, then allowed herself a smile when she thought of how quickly he'd jumped to her aid, no questions asked.

She sat down on the sofa with her nail polish and went to work on her toenails and, switching gears, mulled over the revelations of the conversation with her mother. She understood so much about their relationship now. Could kick herself for not pressing her mom about it sooner. But now she knew. Now she understood and she was going to do something to correct some of the mistakes she'd made that were directly related to those misconceptions.

Starting with Nate. She missed him so much. And she wanted him back. She'd just needed a little time to figure out how she was going to accomplish that.

First, though, she'd had to figure out what she was going to do with the rest of her life. Financially, she was all right for a while. She'd set money aside. She leaned back, extended her legs and admired the Valentine-red color of her toes. She could hold out for a few months until she had to generate some income.

It wasn't that she didn't have any confidence in Nate's ability to help her with the Royal Palms situation, but she'd already decided that on the remote chance they offered to take her back, she wasn't going. If that was the best they could do for her after all she'd given them, it just wasn't good enough.

But *she* was. "I'm good enough, and I'm strong enough and doggone it, I like me," she said with a laugh, paraphrasing lines from an old *Saturday Night Live* skit.

It amazed her, this feeling of euphoria that had grown since she'd worked everything out in her head. She was stronger now. She understood now. And when her security buzzer sounded and the voice on the other end was Nate's, she knew she was ready to face both him and her feelings.

Her heart did a little hopscotch at the sound of his voice. At the prospect of seeing him again. She'd known he was coming—Sylvie had called and warned her. Good thing, too. If he hadn't come to her by today, she was going to him tomorrow.

She buzzed him past security then raced for her bedroom and threw on a pair of white short shorts and a bright-red halter-top. Both new. Both constructed to dazzle. Then she went to work on her hair. It would take him approximately five minutes to drive from the security gate to her front door. She had to work fast.

The old Rachael Matthews would have lobbied for another few days to brace for this meeting and then she would have waded into the water one slow step at a time. The new one wouldn't. The new Rachael planned to dive straight in, the heck with the threat of the undertow. The new Rachael was no longer afraid she'd sink instead of swim.

She knew what she wanted now. Knew what she needed and what she deserved. And she was going to do everything in her power to get it. Starting with tonight.

She ran a quick check of herself in the mirror as her doorbell rang. "You'll do," she told herself with a grin. "You'll do just fine."

Nate had been preparing himself for what he'd find when he finally saw Rachael. He'd talked with Sylvie. He knew how broken Rachael had been when Iverson had suspended her. He remembered the look in her eyes when she'd told him it was over between them. Remembered the defeat in her voice when she called him looking for a lawyer.

She'd been hurting and scared and so vulnerable it made him ache at night. Ache to hold her. Ache to heal her. Ache to love her until all the pain went away.

So he was ready for just about anything when her door swung open—anything but the woman standing there.

"Hi," she said, a smile playing at the corners of her mouth.

"Umm…. Hi."

This woman didn't look beaten. She didn't look bruised. She looked breathless and sassy and as sexy as a siren on an uptown Saturday night.

"Were you planning to come in?" she asked with a playful light in her eye.

*Playful?*

"Are you okay?" he asked cautiously. Something wasn't right here. "Rachael…have you been drinking?"

She actually laughed. "Not a drop. Come in. Please. We need to talk."

"Yeah. That's why I came over. We need to talk about your job."

She shook her head, waved a hand in front of her. "No. I don't want to talk about that. Not yet. I want to talk about us."

"Us?" He felt as if he'd just turtled a Sunfish. The look of her, her mood, her confidence was a total departure from what he expected. And that one little two-letter word buoyed his hopes so high, he had to bring himself back to earth. "Us?" he repeated cautiously. "I thought there *was* no us."

She sobered, took his hand and led him to the sofa where she sat and crossed her bare silky legs beneath her.

"Sit. Please."

"Rachael—"

"No. Wait. I know I don't deserve to have you listen to me. I've been horrible to you and I'm so, so sorry. I need to explain. Can you give that to me? Can you give me the chance to explain a few things?"

He'd give her anything. But he couldn't tell her that just yet. He hadn't been lying the last time he'd seen her and he'd told her everyone was vulnerable. He still felt raw from the way she shoved him out of her town house and out of her life. He wasn't quite ready to lay himself open for her and have her shut him down again.

So he sat back, waited. And he prayed that what she had to tell him was something he wanted to hear.

# Twelve

Rachael watched Nate with her heart in her throat. He was so edgy in his silence, his own heart all but hanging on his sleeve…and she fell a little deeper in love. She wanted to tell him she loved him. But she owed him something else first. An explanation.

"Well," she said, tucking her hair back behind her ear as a second ticked to ten, then ten to twenty. "This is a little harder than I thought it would be."

"What's hard, Rachael?" he asked carefully, and she saw in his eyes that this sudden threat of cold feet on her part was hurting him. And she didn't want to hurt him. Ever.

"Admitting to mistakes. No one likes to make them—especially me—and it's been a real eye-opener to realize I've made more than my fair share. And now I need to own up to them." She stopped, drew a bracing breath. "Bear with me...I'm just going to lay it all out, okay?"

He nodded, his face a mask that suddenly covered his emotions. It was his lawyer face, she realized, about the same time she understood he was still unsure about her feelings for him. And why wouldn't he be? She'd given him nothing to hold on to.

"You...you scared the living daylights out of me." She stopped, smiled. "The first time I saw you...you just made me feel things I told myself I had no business feeling. You are so...so everything I've ever wanted. Everything I was afraid to believe I could have. That's why I tried everything in my power to force you away. But then, you already know that, don't you?"

He took her hand in his, held it tightly and waited.

"What you don't know is why. This is the hard part. This is where I tell you how pathetic I am. Correction. Was. How pathetic I was." She drew another deep breath, let it out. "Okay, just do it, right?"

He squeezed her hands. "Yeah. Just do it."

"I...I've got to go back a ways. Things were tough when I was a kid. My...my dad was...well, let's just say he'd never get father of the year award. My most vivid memories of him were of his fists. And his face...all red, veins bulging as he screamed at my mother. Once...once, he put her in the hospital."

"Rachael—"

She shook her head, clutched his hands tighter. "No. I've got to get this out. Long story short, though, we made a lot of midnight runs to women's shelters before Mom finally got the courage to break out of the cycle and leave him for good. I was nine.

And I still remember the antiseptic smell of those places, the kind, pitying eyes of the volunteers, the wild, vacant stares of the other kids and their moms who had fled for their lives the same way we had."

She drew in another settling breath and, encouraged by the patience in his eyes and the stroke of his thumbs over the back of her hands, continued. "Anyway, we left Ohio and moved here to West Palm. Everything was pretty good for a while and then it got better. Mom met John and fell in love. They got married and I had a real home—a safe home—for the first time in my life. It was perfect."

"So why doesn't it sound so perfect?" he asked gently.

She smiled. Shrugged. "Because it wasn't." She gathered her thoughts and explained. "Mom and John were happy. They started their own family shortly after they got married, and as much as I love the girls, I suddenly became a fifth wheel. Or so I thought at the time.

"This…this is hard," she confessed. "What I have to keep reminding myself is that I was twelve then and I couldn't be expected to understand. All I saw was that after the girls were born, I suddenly wasn't important to her anymore. It was apparent that I was a part of a past she wanted to forget and I didn't have any place in her present or her future."

"But that wasn't really the case, was it?"

She smiled sadly. "What was really happening was that Mom had fallen into a depression. It wasn't just me she turned away from. She turned away from all of us. Poor John. It was all he could do to take care of her and of those babies. I just happened to be old enough to take care of myself. What I wasn't old enough to comprehend was that it wasn't me. This wasn't just happening to me.''

"But it *was* happening to you. And it made you feel unlovable, unwanted and alone.''

She looked up at him, smiled. "Thank you for that. Yes. That's exactly what I felt.''

She thought back to those years when she'd only seen her mom turning her back on her. She was a child. She was twelve, struggling with self-esteem, and all she could feel was the rejection. Her father hadn't loved her. Now her mother didn't love her anymore, either.

"I was so miserable, so certain I wasn't worth loving, that I didn't understand my mother was struggling, too. Cause and effect, I guess, you'd call it. Anyway, I withdrew from her further and further over the years. Even after Mom had her depression under control, the only person I let her see was this self-reliant woman who didn't need her anymore.''

"Because if you didn't need her, she couldn't hurt you, right?''

She compressed her lips, nodded. "So both of us …we just sort of let the distance between us breed and grow, both thinking that was exactly the way we wanted it—when, in truth, we've both been bruised by it.''

She paused again, looked at their joined hands, took heart in the fact that not only had he not pulled away, he held her tighter. "And that leads me to you.''

"I think I've got this part. Your knee-jerk reaction

was that since you were so unlovable, how could I possibly love you? How could anyone love you?''

Feeling sheepish, she nodded. ''Well, I'd racked up a fairly concrete track record to support that theory. Any guy who ever got remotely close—I pushed away when they started making noises about long-term commitment.''

''I could almost feel sorry for them,'' he said.

''Well, don't. I didn't love them. I don't think I ever loved any of them.''

''And now? Now what do you think?''

His eyes were so dark and so full of compassion and longing and love, she thought she'd burst from all the love she felt for him.

''Now I know what love is,'' she said without hesitation. ''Now I know I'd never even been close to it before.''

His eyes warmed to that smile she'd missed every waking and sleeping hour since she'd driven him away. ''How close are you now, Rachael?''

''So close,'' she said, lifting her hand to his chest, where his heart beat steady and true, ''so close I can feel it.''

He covered her hand with his. ''But are you ever going to say it?''

She laughed and fell into his arms. ''I think I just did—when I told you about my childhood. About my problem with trust. It was a big step for me, Mc-Grory.''

''I know.''

''I can't promise that I'll be up front with you all the time. With how I'm feeling. With what I need.''

''I know what you need. You need me. I'm the

man who understands you. I'm the guy who's going to be there, waiting you out when you fold up like a clam. I love you, Rachael. And I'm not going to let you push me away.''

She pulled back so she could see his beautiful face. ''That's what I love about you, McGrory. You don't know when to give up.''

''Not when it comes to you.''

''I love you,'' she whispered, pressing a kiss to his brow. ''I love your smile.'' Another to his lips. ''And your laughter and your strong mind and giving heart.'' She couldn't stop kissing him. ''I love that you're here, in spite of everything I did to drive you away. I love that you haven't walked back out that door and that you let me drone on and on about my dramatic and melodramatic youth—''

He stopped her with a kiss so full of tenderness and caring it brought tears to her eyes. ''Don't minimize what happened to you. Your childhood was traumatic and the fact that you've overcome it to become this strong, stubborn, self-reliant woman only makes me love you more.''

She pressed her forehead to his. ''Thank you. Thank you for not giving up on me.''

''You mean, when you shot me down time and again even after I blew a small fortune on flowers and Mara Lago?''

She smiled and buried her fingers in his hair. ''Yeah, then.''

''When you blackened my eye and bloodied my lip?''

''Umm. Yeah.'' She touched her fingertips lovingly

to the corner of his mouth. "You're not going to let go of that anytime soon, are you?"

"What I'm not going to let go of, is you."

"Promise?"

"Promise. You may have been unlucky in love in the past Ms. Matthews, but from this point on consider yourself the luckiest woman alive in that department."

"Does this mean I'm going to get lucky tonight?"

He laughed and, pressing her down into the sofa cushions, started tugging the strap of her halter top down her shoulder. "I'd say," he whispered against the breast he'd bared and sent a shiver sluicing through her, "you're about to get very, very lucky."

"So…maybe it was all supposed to happen like this," Rachael said later, rousing Nate from a hazy half sleep as they lay in the soft darkness of her bedroom. She lifted her head and propped it on her hands, which she'd stacked on his chest.

She felt so good sprawled on top of him. Her softness to his hard angles. Her sensitive breasts to his chest. "Could be," he agreed, running his hands up and down the length of her body, loving the feel of her bare skin beneath his hands, lingering at the curve of her bottom to press her against him.

They'd made love and talked and made love again. He'd told her about Tia and how it had taken meeting her to make him realize he had never really loved Tia.

"Oh…almost forgot," he said lazily. "I got your job back."

She reared back, bracing her palms on his chest.

"You got my job back?" she asked, incredulous, then laughed. "How?"

He drew her back against him, nipped at her shoulder. "The same way everything works in Palm Beach society. I made some calls to some key people and sang your praises, and they in turn sang your praises to some of Mrs. Buckley's Angels of Charity cohorts who put the screws to Mrs. B and voilà—to save face, she made some of her own calls and asked that you be reinstated."

She cupped his face in her hands. "Amazing. Thank you. Thank you for doing that for me. Now, how upset are you going to be when I tell you I don't want to go back to Royal Palms?"

"Because you deserved better from them than they gave you?"

"Damn straight."

He laughed and hugged her hard. "Somehow, I figured that stubborn streak might come into play, so I made sure the hotel offered up a contingency settlement to make up for the defamation of character, loss of salary, pain and suffering, and whatever else I could think of to throw in there."

She laughed. "Pain and suffering. I like that part."

"You're going to like this part even better." He named the figure the hotel had coughed up in an effort to avoid the lawsuit he had assured them he'd be filing on Rachael's behalf.

"Holy cow!" She sat straight up this time, straddling him in all her naked glory. She looked so pretty and pink and so damn sexy he had to wrestle her to her back again and take advantage of all the gratitude she felt compelled to bestow on him.

"I want what Tony has," he whispered an hour or so later.

She snuggled against his side and yawning, threw a bare leg over his thighs. "I think that's called sibling rivalry."

He loved it that she was secure in his love for her. "It's called I want it all, Rachael. I want to marry you."

She hiked herself up on an elbow, her eyes shining like emeralds in the night. "Doesn't that work out well...I just happen to know where you can get a really great wedding planner. And for you, I think she'd work out a real sweet deal."

"I've already got a sweet deal." As sweet as the lips that met his.

"And I'm the luckiest woman in the world."

"I'm going to take that as a yes. Yes?"

"You are definitely going to take that as a yes." She kissed him again. "Yes." And again. "Yes." And again before she settled back against his side with a contented sigh and punctuated her final affirmation with a jubilant raised fist. "Yes!"

# Epilogue

**W**ell, Rachael thought as Sylvie made final adjustments to her train in preparation for her walk down the aisle—*this* wasn't supposed to happen. She was *not* supposed to be worrying over details. Sylvie, her partner in Miami's newest bridal-consulting business, Miami Brides, had been planning this wedding for six months, step by meticulous step to make sure it was perfect.

And so far, it was.

It was as perfect as the man waiting for her at the altar with the smile that had stolen her heart the first time he'd flashed it her way.

Love. For her. It shone in Nate's flashing brown eyes as he stood in his black cutaway tux with his brother and Sam by his side.

Love. For him. It filled Rachael to bursting as she

clutched her bridal bouquet and walked on her step-father's arm to her destiny. Love. For her mom who, during the past several months, had laughed with her and cried with her and in the process they had found their way back to each other.

*You're beautiful,* Nate McGrory's speaking eyes told her with a tenderness that made her heart sing. *Come, mi corazón. Let's get these vows over with so I can officially say you're mine.*

She hoped her eyes did a little speaking, too. *I have always been yours. I will always be yours.*

She would remember every moment of this day. Her mother's pride. Karen and Kimmie in lavender-rose, smiling through their own tears that told her how happy they were for. Her sisters and Nate's family embracing their special day.

But what she would remember most of all was the look in her husband's eyes as he held her in his arms that night and filled her with a tender passion that made her heart sing.

"I love you, Rachael. Now. Always. Forever."

Lucky, she thought as she lost herself in his love. How did I ever get so lucky in love?

\*    \*    \*    \*    \*

✂ **Your opinion is important to us!** Please take a few moments to share your thoughts with us about your experiences with Harlequin and Silhouette books. Your comments will be very useful in ensuring that we deliver books you love to read. *Please take a few minutes to complete the questionnaire, then send it to us at the address below.*

Send your completed questionnaires to:
**Harlequin/Silhouette Reader Survey, P.O. Box 9046, Buffalo, NY 14269-9046**

1. As you may know, there are many different lines under the Harlequin and Silhouette brands. Each of the lines is listed below. Please check the box that most represents your reading habit for each line.

| Line | Currently read this line | Do not read this line | Not sure if I read this line |
|---|---|---|---|
| Harlequin American Romance | ❏ | ❏ | ❏ |
| Harlequin Duets | ❏ | ❏ | ❏ |
| Harlequin Romance | ❏ | ❏ | ❏ |
| Harlequin Historicals | ❏ | ❏ | ❏ |
| Harlequin Superromance | ❏ | ❏ | ❏ |
| Harlequin Intrigue | ❏ | ❏ | ❏ |
| Harlequin Presents | ❏ | ❏ | ❏ |
| Harlequin Temptation | ❏ | ❏ | ❏ |
| Harlequin Blaze | ❏ | ❏ | ❏ |
| Silhouette Special Edition | ❏ | ❏ | ❏ |
| Silhouette Romance | ❏ | ❏ | ❏ |
| Silhouette Intimate Moments | ❏ | ❏ | ❏ |
| Silhouette Desire | ❏ | ❏ | ❏ |

2. Which of the following best describes why you bought *this book*? One answer only, please.

| | | | |
|---|---|---|---|
| the picture on the cover | ❏ | the title | ❏ |
| the author | ❏ | the line is one I read often | ❏ |
| part of a miniseries | ❏ | saw an ad in another book | ❏ |
| saw an ad in a magazine/newsletter | ❏ | a friend told me about it | ❏ |
| I borrowed/was given this book | ❏ | other: _____ | ❏ |

3. Where did you buy *this book*? One answer only, please.

| | | | |
|---|---|---|---|
| at Barnes & Noble | ❏ | at a grocery store | ❏ |
| at Waldenbooks | ❏ | at a drugstore | ❏ |
| at Borders | ❏ | on eHarlequin.com Web site | ❏ |
| at another bookstore | ❏ | from another Web site | ❏ |
| at Wal-Mart | ❏ | Harlequin/Silhouette Reader | ❏ |
| at Target | ❏ | Service/through the mail | |
| at Kmart | ❏ | used books from anywhere | ❏ |
| at another department store or mass merchandiser | ❏ | I borrowed/was given this book | ❏ |

4. On average, how many Harlequin and Silhouette books do you buy at one time?

| | |
|---|---|
| I buy _____ books at one time | ❏ |
| I rarely buy a book | ❏ |

MRQ403SD-1A

5. How many times per month do you shop for any *Harlequin and/or Silhouette* books? One answer only, please.

| | | | |
|---|---|---|---|
| 1 or more times a week | ❑ | a few times per year | ❑ |
| 1 to 3 times per month | ❑ | less often than once a year | ❑ |
| 1 to 2 times every 3 months | ❑ | never | ❑ |

6. When you think of your ideal heroine, which *one* statement describes her the best? One answer only, please.

| | | | |
|---|---|---|---|
| She's a woman who is strong-willed | ❑ | She's a desirable woman | ❑ |
| She's a woman who is needed by others | ❑ | She's a powerful woman | ❑ |
| She's a woman who is taken care of | ❑ | She's a passionate woman | ❑ |
| She's an adventurous woman | ❑ | She's a sensitive woman | ❑ |

7. The following statements describe types or genres of books that you may be interested in reading. Pick *up to 2 types* of books that you are most interested in.

| | |
|---|---|
| I like to read about truly romantic relationships | ❑ |
| I like to read stories that are sexy romances | ❑ |
| I like to read romantic comedies | ❑ |
| I like to read a romantic mystery/suspense | ❑ |
| I like to read about romantic adventures | ❑ |
| I like to read romance stories that involve family | ❑ |
| I like to read about a romance in times or places that I have never seen | ❑ |
| Other: _____ | ❑ |

*The following questions help us to group your answers with those readers who are similar to you. Your answers will remain confidential.*

8. Please record your year of birth below.

19 ____

9. What is your marital status?

single ❑     married ❑     common-law ❑     widowed ❑
divorced/separated ❑

10. Do you have children 18 years of age or younger currently living at home?

yes ❑     no ❑

11. Which of the following best describes your employment status?

employed full-time or part-time ❑     homemaker ❑     student ❑
retired ❑     unemployed ❑

12. Do you have access to the Internet from either home or work?

yes ❑     no ❑

13. Have you ever visited eHarlequin.com?

yes ❑     no ❑

14. What state do you live in?

_____

15. Are you a member of Harlequin/Silhouette Reader Service?

yes ❑     Account # _____     no ❑     MRQ403SD-1B

If you enjoyed what you just read,
then we've got an offer you can't resist!

# Take 2 bestselling
# love stories FREE!

# Plus get a FREE surprise gift!

**Clip this page and mail it to Silhouette Reader Service™**

| IN U.S.A. | IN CANADA |
|---|---|
| 3010 Walden Ave. | P.O. Box 609 |
| P.O. Box 1867 | Fort Erie, Ontario |
| Buffalo, N.Y. 14240-1867 | L2A 5X3 |

**YES!** Please send me 2 free Silhouette Desire® novels and my free surprise gift. After receiving them, if I don't wish to receive anymore, I can return the shipping statement marked cancel. If I don't cancel, I will receive 6 brand-new novels every month, before they're available in stores! In the U.S.A., bill me at the bargain price of $3.57 plus 25¢ shipping and handling per book and applicable sales tax, if any*. In Canada, bill me at the bargain price of $4.24 plus 25¢ shipping and handling per book and applicable taxes**. That's the complete price and a savings of at least 10% off the cover prices—what a great deal! I understand that accepting the 2 free books and gift places me under no obligation ever to buy any books. I can always return a shipment and cancel at any time. Even if I never buy another book from Silhouette, the 2 free books and gift are mine to keep forever.

225 SDN DNUP
326 SDN DNUQ

| Name | (PLEASE PRINT) | |
|---|---|---|
| Address | Apt.# | |
| City | State/Prov. | Zip/Postal Code |

\* Terms and prices subject to change without notice. Sales tax applicable in N.Y.
\*\* Canadian residents will be charged applicable provincial taxes and GST.
 All orders subject to approval. Offer limited to one per household and not valid to
 current Silhouette Desire® subscribers.
 ® are registered trademarks of Harlequin Books S.A., used under license.

DES02 ©1998 Harlequin Enterprises Limited

**From**
# Katherine Garbera

# CINDERELLA'S CHRISTMAS AFFAIR

**Silhouette Desire #1546**

With the help of a matchmaking
angel in training, two ugly-ducklings-
turned-swans experience passion and
love…and a little holiday magic.

## You're on his hit list.

*Available November 2003
at your favorite retail outlet.*

# COMING NEXT MONTH

**#1543  WITH PRIVATE EYES—Eileen Wilks**
*Dynasties: The Barones*
Socialite Claudia Barone *insisted* on helping investigate the attempted
sabotage of her family's business. But detective Ethan Mallory had a
hard head to match his hard body. He always worked on his own....he
didn't need the sexy sophisticate on the case. What he *wanted*...well,
that was another matter!

**#1544  BABY, YOU'RE MINE—Peggy Moreland**
*The Tanners of Texas*
In one moment, Woodrow Tanner changed Dr. Elizabeth Montgomery's life.
The gruff-yet-sexy rancher had come bearing news of her estranged sister's
death—and the existence of Elizabeth's baby niece. Even as Elizabeth tried
to accept this startling news, she couldn't help but crave Woodrow's consoling
embrace....

**#1545  WILD IN THE FIELD—Jennifer Greene**
*The Lavender Trilogy*
Like the fields of lavender growing outside her window, Camille Campbell
looked sweet and delicate, but could thrive even in the harshest conditions.
Divorced dad and love-wary neighbor Pete MacDougal found in Camille a
kindred soul...whose body could elicit in him the most amazing feelings....

**#1546  CINDERELLA'S CHRISTMAS AFFAIR—Katherine Garbera**
*King of Hearts*
Brawny businessman Tad Randolph promised his parents he'd be married
with children before Christmas—and cool-as-ice executive CJ Terrance was
the perfect partner for his pretend wedding and baby-making scheme. But
soon Tad realized she was more fire than ice...and found himself wishing
CJ shared more than just his bed!

**#1547  ENTANGLED WITH A TEXAN—Sara Orwig**
*Texas Cattleman's Club: The Stolen Baby*
A certain sexy rancher was the stuff of fantasies for baby store clerk
Marissa Wilder. So when David Sorrenson showed up needing Marissa's
help, she quickly agreed to be a temporary live-in nanny for the mystery baby
David was caring for. But could she convince her fantasy man to care for *her*,
as well?

**#1548  AWAKENING BEAUTY—Amy J. Fetzer**
There was more to dowdy bookseller Lane Douglas than met the eye...and
Tyler McKay was determined to find out her secrets. Resisting the magnetic
millionaire was difficult for Lane, but she vowed to keep her identity under
wraps...even as her heart and body threatened to betray her.

SDCNM1003